WILLOWCREEK DISCIPLE

KEVIN BROOKS

© Copyright 2006 Kevin Brooks
All rights reserved. No part of this publication may be reproduced, stored in a retrieval system, or transmitted, in any form or by any means, electronic, mechanical, photocopying, recording, or otherwise, without the written prior permission of the author.

Note for Librarians: A cataloguing record for this book is available from Library and Archives Canada at www.collectionscanada.ca/amicus/index-e.html
ISBN 1-4251-0734-6

Printed in Victoria, BC, Canada. Printed on paper with minimum 30% recycled fibre. Trafford's print shop runs on "green energy" from solar, wind and other environmentally-friendly power sources.

TRAFFORD
PUBLISHING
Offices in Canada, USA, Ireland and UK

Book sales for North America and international:
Trafford Publishing, 6E–2333 Government St.,
Victoria, BC V8T 4P4 CANADA
phone 250 383 6864 (toll-free 1 888 232 4444)
fax 250 383 6804; email to orders@trafford.com
Book sales in Europe:
Trafford Publishing (UK) Limited, 9 Park End Street, 2nd Floor
Oxford, UK OX1 1HH UNITED KINGDOM
phone +44 (0)1865 722 113 (local rate 0845 230 9601)
facsimile +44 (0)1865 722 868; info.uk@trafford.com
Order online at:
trafford.com/06-2492

10 9 8 7 6 5 4 3 2

TABLE OF CONTENTS

CHAPTER 1	THE HOMECOMING	9
CHAPTER 2	THE PLOT and PAYBACK	23
CHAPTER 3	RETALIATION and THE HEIST	41
CHAPTER 4	INDECENT PROPOSAL	55
CHAPTER 5	FUNERAL TURNED MORGUE	67
CHAPTER 6	LIFE-ALTERING DREAM	77
CHAPTER 7	END TIMES	103

PLUS… a Condensed
Ebonics
DICTIONARY

This book is dedicated to the loving memory of Marque Taylor who encouraged and gave me the confidence to complete it. This one's for you, Homie. Also, to Grandpa Brooks, Roddy Thompson, Terry Henderson, Yusavio Patterson (Playa), Billy Steptoe, Jerry Thompson, GooGoo and Mortimar George. Last but not least, this book is dedicated to my beautiful Grandma Brooks, who believed in my writing abilities and subsequently sponsored this whole project. This is for all of y'all because you all inspired me to keep on writing. Rest in Peace.

This book in its entirety is fictitious. If any of the events in this book seem to be similar to any real life occurrences, then that is totally coincidental. Again I reiterate that this novel is a figment of the author's imagination. So with that said, I now introduce to you Willowcreek Disciple....

A Kevin Brooks creation...

WILLOWCREEK DISCIPLE...

A Kevin Brooks creation...

INTRODUCTION

These are the events which led to the demise of a small criminal enterprise. A group of six young thugs made up the Willowcreek posse. The name derived from their apartment complex, Willowcreek apartments. All were between the ages of twenty through twenty-three and had had their run-ins with the law and other thugs affiliated with other gangs. The members went by the name of Tank, Playa, Pop, Solo, Suga, and Pookie. For the most part, they had known each other for most of their lives.

The leader of the posse was Tank, a twenty-three-year-old smooth talker and dresser. Now Tank was one of those brothers that over-ambitious young brothers wanted to be like. He had the women, money and clothes. He was handsome, charming, and when worst came to worst, ruthless. The only blemish he had on his record was a trafficking and possession charge of marijuana and crack. Since he would not reveal his supplier, the judge had given Tank a five-year sentence, of which three years and a day he had served. When he was out of prison and back on the streets, he was considered a true gangster, and the younger gangsters revered him. I guess this promotion into the world of crime made Tank take it upon himself to run his own crew. Tank was originally from New York City, but he moved to Houston with his mom when he was ten years old, so he considered himself a Houstonian. However, being born in the Big Apple, he felt that he had to live up to a reputation of being a hardcore big city boy. When Tank first moved to Houston, Playa was the first friend he had made. That is why people were under the impression that the two were brothers. If one saw Tank, Playa was usually in the vicinity.

Playa was the next in charge of the delinquents. Playa was a twenty-one-year-old thug, who, as you can tell by his name, was quite a ladies man. He believed that he was a hustler by nature. In a strange way, he believed that he was justified of all his actions. After all, he often said, "My old man is dead, plus I'm only a product of my environment; if I don't hustle, then I don't eat." His dad had died of an aneurysm, excessive drinking being the main contributor. For that reason, Playa despised anyone who let alcohol take control of their lives, and he took on a father-figure roll in his household.

Pop was a twenty-year-old quick-tempered thug who had problems restraining his mouth. He had first been institutionalized at fourteen years old, and ever since then, he had been going in and out of the judiciary revolving door. He was always fighting; even if he knew that the odds were against him, he was still willing to fight. He was a valuable member of the crew because he was always willing to scuffle. If he was told to rough up another thug, he always agreed. He was the sort of person who thrived on confrontations. Don't get me wrong, Pop was a cool brother, but if you crossed him or even got in his way, it was on.

Solo would most likely introduce himself by asking, "Where the weed at?" Solo was the twenty-one-year-old ex-football, ex-basketball, and ex-baseball player. He got high for the first time at sixteen years old, and ever since then, he was always high. Solo was first a lover, and then a fighter. It wasn't that he could not fight, but he was always busy with a female companion. His main girl was Roketta, but she didn't deter him from having other lady friends. He was even more of a player than Playa. If any of his comrades wanted a female, they would just call him because he knew plenty.

Suga was a twenty-one-year-old thug. He was the sticky finger of the posse. He and Playa were first cousins; in actuality, they had been brought up like brothers rather than cousins. Their maternal grandmother had raised them both since they could remember. Suga was actually a couple of months older than Playa, but Playa was always the stronger of the two, so he looked on Suga as his younger brother.

Pookie was the twenty-two-year-old comedian, slash peacemaker of the crew. Pookie was down with Willowcreek posse, but he had family all over Houston, so he was also down with people who were not down with Willowcreek posse. He wasn't an official member of the gang, but he was always around them. So a lot of people thought that he was affiliated with them. For the main part, the others let Pookie hang around because he was always making someone laugh. He had a knack for talking about people in a joking manner, also known as ranking, and that was a valuable attribute to possess in the ghetto.

CHAPTER 1

THE HOMECOMING

It was a muggy and humid evening. The rain seemed to vacuum the oxygen out of the atmosphere. The mosquitoes were bad, but swats were the preferred defense down south. The humidity and mosquitoes were bad, but in the poverty- stricken ghetto known as Willowcreek, all was well. You still saw the winos hanging out in front of the liquor store. The little kids buying goodies from the ice cream truck. The homeboys playing tackle football in the streets. The drug dealers selling death in the park - that's where Playa worked. He worked about six hours a day, and that day was no exception. He was there with Pop, hustling illegally. Pop said to Playa as he counted his money, "Man, I just need one hundred more dollars to get that Nike suit." Playa replied, "Which one, that black one?"

"You know it," Pop answered with a smile. "I got to look good for those females."

Pop and Playa continued to talk, not realizing that they had turned their backs to the get-away route. You know, the hole in the fence that they ran through if the police or enemy came.

Without warning, someone creeped through the fence while their backs were still turned. A voice said ecstatically, "The dead has risen my niggas!" Can you sense the picture? Playa and Pop were seeing Tank on the streets for the first time in a little over three years. Playa asked, almost shouting, "When you got out, my nigga?" Tank answered, embracing the two thugs, "Man y'all the first familiar faces that I'm seeing. I just not came out." Pop laughed and nodded his head, "Dog, you must have been doing some serious weightlifting, because you done got swole." The three seemed to be getting emotional when Tank interrupted, "Lookit here, I'm just coming out of prison. If them boys creep up on me right now, I'll be going right back to Huntsville prison. I'm getting out of here. Is y'all coming?"

Playa answered, almost disappointed, "How you gonna ask us that? You know we're coming', dog."

As they exited the drug dealers' paradise, Tank spotted Solo across the street in the middle of a crap game (dice game). Tank pointed as he asked, "Is that the homie, Solo?" Playa answered while walking towards the game, "Yeah, that's that nigga."

Pop said, "I bet you that that fool is high."

Playa replied, "You already know that if he ain't high, something got to be wrong."

As they continued to walk, Tank couldn't help but to yell, "I got fifty dollars on you, my nigga." When Solo realized that it was Tank, he walked away with the dice to properly hale him. His two opponents were irritated at the disruption, and told him to hurry up and roll the dice. Wrong move. For one, he was just giving respect to his friend he had not seen in three years, and secondly, the four most explosive of the posse were together. You could see the vengeance in Pop's eyes as he said, "Shut up fools, or else I'll take all of your money!" One of the wanna-be hustlers answered back; "Man, you must be crazy."

Before you realized it, Pop was on top of the smart mouth hustler, swinging punches. Playa and Solo invited themselves into the squabble.

As those three roughed up the first young hustler, Tank walked over to the second one. "You know me boy?"

"Naw," he answered.

"I'll tell you who I am. I'm Tank and I'm the new sheriff in town. Since your home boy has such a big mouth, you have to pay in order not to get treated like he is."

The young hustler glanced at his friend and saw that the three thugs were mangling him. "I haven't even said nothing," he tried to protest.

Tank reinstated firmly with his hand extended, "That's the rules, boy." After he confiscated the money, he walked over to the first hustler and broke up the beating, "For a little nigga, you sure do got a big mouth. You live around here fool?"

The hustler answered after he wiped off the blood from his newly-swollen lips, "Yeah."

Tank continued, "These are our streets now. Order has come back to Willowcreek, and we're here to enforce it. Here's the deal, we're your new bodyguards, and our services cost a hundred dollars a week."

The hustler objected, "I don't need a bodyguard."

Tank reinstated while slapping him in the face, "By the looks of it, you need a bodyguard now. I want a hundred dollars every Monday, and if I don't get it, you're gonna know why they call me Tank. You heard?"

The beat up hustler reluctantly answered Tank, "Yeah."

When the two hustlers left the scene, Solo began to laugh, "This is why I missed you, Homie. Your presence alone hypes the brothers up" The two properly greeted each other as they originally intended to before they were rudely interrupted.

"Did you just come out?" Solo asked. Again, Tank answered, "Yeah, a nigga done just came out."

Solo asked, "Have you seen Tameka yet?"

"Naw man, I had to peep the homies first," Tank answered while counting the confiscated money.

"Forget Tameka. I'm gonna introduce you to Tina, that's a bad girl there. man," Solo said before he whistled.

Pop said, "Nigga, you ought to be a pimp; you know all them gals."

Solo boasted, "I just got game, son."

Playas cross-examined, "Not more than me."

"Dog you must done lost your mind! My gals is on point," Solo said as he opened his eyes wide.

"What gals? Them old chicken heads?" Playa objected. Tank let himself into the conversation. "I ain't had one girl in three years, and y'all is over here bragging about which one of y'all got the freshest girl. Y'all niggas be quiet man."

Pop said, "Ooh."

Tank glanced at Pop. "You be quiet too, nigga!"

Pop, consciously defying Tank's order, asked Solo, "You got your ride fixed Solo?"

"Yeah, why?"

Pop, feeling the money in his pocket, said, "Let's go to the mall y'all."

"I ain't got no real money man," Tank said.

Pop replied, "Don't worry, dog, I got your back."

Solo and Playa also agreed to treat Tank to a new wardrobe, because his old one was outdated.

The local mall was called Bluepoints Mall. It was a known hangout for Bluepoints posse, a rival gang. Bluepoints and Willowcreek posse had had their clashes in the past.

The two apartment complexes were near in geographical areas, maybe five miles apart, but as far as love for each other, the gang members were many miles away. Willowcreek posse was the stronger of the two gangs; in fact, they were one of the strongest young gangs in northeast Houston at the time. They were known because, for the most part, they wore green shirts with dark pants. Bluepoints posse, for obvious reasons, wore blue shirts with dark blue pants. They were known to get gung-ho at times, but Willowcreek posse considered them inferior.

Upon arrival at the mall, the four thugs saw five of the Bluepoints members staring at them as if they were on the wrong turf. Pop was the first of the four thugs to respond.

"What's wrong with them fools, dog? They staring at us like we crippled or something."

Tank told his comrades, "Man, forget them niggas; they ain't about nothing. Let's just get what we came to get, and be out."

They ignored the stares, and decided to go to Footlockers, to get the latest fashion in footwear. They each got a brand new pair of sneakers, and bought clothes to revitalize their gang uniforms. They browsed around in the mall, and as usual, Solo and Playa got a couple of telephone numbers from a couple different ladies. They finally decided to leave the mall after about an hour and a half.

While the four were walking towards Solo's car, they didn't notice the young men walking towards them.

"Get down niggas, down, down, down!!!" A van on the side of the curb was the nest for the robbers. There must have been at least eight members of the Bluepoints posse who held different weapons. I saw at least four guns, but the ambush was set up so perfectly, that there was nothing the four could do. It all took place in less than a minute. As they were running back towards the get-away car, Tank shouted, "Watch your backs, punks!" One of the robbers holding a gun pointed it towards Tank and squeezed the trigger twice. Luckily for Tank, the gun was jammed, and when Willowcreek realized this, they all ran away. The van also left the scene of the crime.

They were all furious as well as humiliated. Tank said,
"It's on now! Them fools done lit a match in the kitchen. I was trying to be nice, now look what they started, ol' stupid niggas!" All of them agreed that Bluepoints posse had started some beef, and it was time to burn them. However, it could not be on that night, because they didn't have the weapons to retaliate.

When the posse arrived in their own neighborhood, it was as if they felt that they were extortionists, and would shake down some local business, but again Tank went against the tactics of the other three. They wanted revenge immediately. Pop said, "Man, let's go and get them punk niggas!"

Solo joined in, "Yeah, let's get them niggas. I ain't never felt so weak!" Playa agreed also. "I'm down with that." Tank weighed the pro's and con's, similar to a quarter back on a football team, and decided that if they scrambled too soon, they would be sacked for a bigger lost. "I feel y'all man, but let's get them on the sneak tip. They'll be expecting us to come back tonight, so let's keep them wondering for a little while, and when the time is right, then we'll strike."

Playa agreed, "You're right, Homie. Let's catch them unprepared."

A declaration of war was unannounced, but obviously declared against Bluepoints posse. Willowcreek posse was determined to use some stealth bomber tactics against their arch-enemies. The four decided to go their separate ways, but agreed to get back together later that night. Playa and Tank chose to stick together, and go to Playa's house to play some video games.

When they reached Playa's house, Playa's grandmother was in the living room, reading her bible. Playa whispered to Tank, "Damn man, she's gonna preach to us."

Tank answered while laughing, "I can predict that; Mama ain't changed a bit."

Grandma looked towards the door, and noticed that it was Playa and one of his friends. "Which one of your friends is that, Tarrance?" Tank answered her, "It's me, Mama, Frank."

Grandma said, "Frank you finally came home! How are you doing son?"

Tank answered, trying to avoid a long discussion, "I'm alright Mama."

Grandma urged the boys, "Y'all come sit here; let me talk to y'all."

"Mama, we're gonna play some video games first," Playa said, trying to avoid the lecture.

Grandma answered in a stern voice, "You think those video games can save you from going to hell? Y'all come sit here!" There was no other alternative; the two thugs would have to hear Grandma out for at least a few minutes.

Grandma started the conversation by asking, "What y'all boys plan on doing with your lives?" Neither of the boys volunteered to share their ambitions with her. "I tell you what," she continued while taking off her eyeglasses, "y'all must wanna be like them gangsters that I see on the news, that sells his soul to the devil to gain the filthy riches of this world, and in the process, breaks everybody's heart around him. Don't y'all know that y'all be breaking y'all mama's heart?"

Tank was angered at the thought of his mother. "Not mine."

"That's besides the point, baby," she said as she rebounded the conversation. "Y'all still be breaking other people's hearts, and plus you making a deal with the devil. Sure he'll give you the world, but in the end he's gonna have the rights to your soul in hell. Can you even imagine going to hell eternally? I know that you cannot, because I can't and I am seventy-two-years-old.

I tell you boys something. These is the last days we're living in. Can't y'all realize that there's so many deceptions out there? Uh huh, you can be living politically correct, but still on your way to hell. All you have to do is ask JESUS into your heart, and he will forgive you, no matter what you do."

Playa, noticeably irritated, said, "I ain't trying to hear nothing about JESUS. I already told you that that's a white man's religion devised to keep the black man in submission."

Grandma replied gently, as if anticipating this response,

"Baby, I already told you that JESUS is neither black, white, Spanish, Chinese, or even, Portuguese. The bible says that 'those that worship Me must worship Me in spirit and in truth.' Therefore, you can throw away your white and black pictures of JESUS, because they are both inaccurate, and if anyone claims to be a Christian, and he or she is a racist, they are deceived. GOD is love and he loves everyone no matter the race of the person."

Playa answered skeptically, "Mama, believe what you want to believe, but I still believe that the black man is god." Grandma continued, "Lookit here, if you go to anyone's grave, you'll see them there, and the same thing goes with any other self- proclaimed god, but if you go to JESUS' grave, you won't see him because he has risen, and now sits on the right hand of the Father."

Tank asked Grandma sincerely, "I don't know, Mama - if he's so loving then why does he let bad things happen to good people?"

She continued, "Good question, now do you really think that he wants bad things to happen to us? Think about it - that's like a parent wanting something bad to happen to their child. In the beginning, GOD created Adam and Eve and told them to be fruitful and multiply. Then they sinned and as a result, a curse was handed down to them and their seeds. We are now living under this same curse. The first murder committed, was when Cain killed Abel, because he was jealous of him, and GOD is so loving that he spared Cain's life, because his nature is forgiving. I know that this is a cold world, but GOD didn't intend it to be like this."

Just then, there was a knock at the door. Playa was happy for the interruption. "Excuse me, Mama, I'm going to see who it is."

When Playa reached the door he asked, "Who that?" The voice at the other end of the door replied, "It's me, man. I forgot my keys." Playa recognized the voice to be his cousin, Suga. When he opened up, he saw that Pookie accompanied him. The two brothers greeted Playa as they entered the apartment. "What's up dogs?" Playa responded. The two also greeted Grandma; that's when they spotted Tank. "Yo what's up my nigga? You finally done came out!" Suga said almost screaming. Grandma barged into the homecoming, "Watch your mouth, boy! Where you think you at?"

Suga answered back in an argumentative tone, "Why you trippin, Mama? I ain't said one cuss word."

Pookie joined into the welcoming committee, consciously watching the use of the word "nigga". "What's up, homeboy?"

Tank answered the questions directed to him. "Man I'm just chilling. I just got out, and already me and Playa is getting schooled by Mama."

Playa gladly barged into the welcoming. "Hey, dogs, let's go outside and reminisce some more." Suga knew that Playa was trying to elude one of Grandma's sermons and so he said, "Alright man."

Suga continued, "Mama, we'll be back in a while."

As she was getting up from the table, Grandma said, "Y'all be careful out there, and please don't commit no crimes." They all agreed with Mama, knowing that if she thought they were lying, she would preach on continuously.

"Damn man, Grandma be getting out of hand with that preaching stuff," Playa said, obviously still disturbed by the old lady's witnessing.

"I know man, she be tripping," Suga answered back.

"Yo, at least she care about y'all," Tank said, taking their complaints as ungratefulness.

"Dog, you don't even understand. We hear this kind of talk everyday; it's like we be in church everyday," Playa continued to debate. Tank said, "Some of what she be talking about be making sense." Playa asked while smiling, "So what nigga? Is you gonna become a Christian?"

Tank answered back on Grandma's behalf, "I ain't said all of that. I'm just saying a lot of what she was talking about made sense. But on a different note," he continued, "them niggas from Bluepoints crossed the line today, so now we got to get them back for jacking us. Is y'all niggas down with that are what?"

Pookie asked, "Them niggas had the nerves to rob y'all?" Playa answered him directly, "Yea fool, we got to hit them niggas up and return the favor."

Pookie asked, as if to take the blame away from Bluepoints posse, "How do you know that it was them?"

Playa looked at him with a serious face. "What you think I can't see now? If I said it was them then it was them, nigga. Them dummies didn't even wear no masks."

Suga asked Tank, "So where did they jack y'all at?"

"Man, me, Playa, Solo, and Pop just bought some stuff at the mall, and them niggas jumped out of a van with gats and knives, and just jacked us. That nigga Detric even tried to cap me, but his gun jammed."

Suga was amazed at their boldness. "Yea, man, we got to get them niggas. They don't even have heart. I bet that them niggas was smoked out."

Tank agreed. "Yeah, them niggas had to be smoked out."

Pop and Solo lit a joint while they were selling drugs in the park, to recompense for their misfortunes earlier in the day. Since they were under the influence, they were paranoid carrying out their evil endeavor. Pop asked Solo while he was looking across the street, "Who that dude over there is? I ain't never saw him before."

Solo answered, " I know that cat; he ain't about nothing." Pop, still not satisfied with the answer, said, " I'm saying, why he staring over here like he wants to rob us or something?"

Solo, laughing at Pop's paranoia, answered, " Naw, man, why you trippin? Trust me, that fool ain't about nothing. I know him." The two were in the park for about forty-five minutes when Pop received a page with a code from Playa's number. The code signified that they should meet-up at the gambling house.

They immediately responded to Playa's calling of them and left the park. When they met with the rest of the guys, everybody greeted each other. The tone of the conversation was definitely unpleasant. It was as if they were looking for trouble and had found it. Of course, Pop was the instigator. "Ain't that Roketta walking out of the store with another nigga?" Solo quickly turned his head in the direction of the store. "I'll be back." He waited for the jeep to pass before he crossed the street with a bad-boy strut. The other five followed him across the street as if to give him moral support. Roketta saw Solo, and noticed the look in his eyes; it was one of his ' I'm about to start trouble' looks.

Solo pushed Roketta to the side and confronted the flashy dressed stud with her. "What you doing man? This is my gal." The pretty boy noticed the other five gangsters. "Naw, man, I'm just talking to her." Solo spit on the ground before he said, "I don't know you, fool, so you're not allowed to talk to my gal." The flashy dressed ladies' man, who looked to be about twenty, answered back by saying, " I didn't know, man. I was just asking her a question." Roketta barged into the conversation by saying, "I can talk to people; I ain't your property!"

Solo said, "Shut up, girl. I ain't talking to you yet." He directed his attention back to the guy. "You lying, man." Spontaneously, Solo swung two punches. He hit the pretty boy with a left to the ribs, and a right to the jaw. That was all the punches that were needed for this particular fight. Solo remembered the seizure of his property earlier, so that only boosted him to strip the semi-conscious victim of all his valuables. He took his money, jewelry and his brand new pair of Jordan's.

After this, Solo grabbed Roketta by her wrist and yelled, "What you think you doing, Girl?" She was desperately trying to free herself. "What? I can't talk to no guys, but you can have your whore friends?" Solo loosened his grip on her as he said, "Why you always got to bring that up? We ain't talking about me now. I don't ever want to see you with another nigga that I don't know."

She looked directly in his eyes and said, "I don't care what you want." Immediately he gave her a mediocre shove, and demanded that she was to go home. She tried to put up a resistance, but to no avail. In the end, she went home, feeling that she was somehow the cause of the fight. The beat up Don

Juan was allowed to leave, after the other members chucked him around first.

This was the night that Tank, Playa, Pop, Solo and Suga had "Willowcreek Posse" tattooed on their chests as a sign of their loyalty to each other. It was the night that these five young men vowed to elevate the violence that they were known for.

It was two months since Tank had been out of prison, and the posse did more in that time than they had done in the previous three years prior to his homecoming. The crew did a little bit of everything to earn money, but drug dealing was their preference. The five hoodlums expanded their drug-trafficking area. They not only dealt from the park, but they also made deals in Mexico. Tank had met this Colombian guy who was well-connected, called Santiago, in prison. He had taken a liking to the way Tank carried himself, so he promised that once they both were on the outside, they could do business together. He got out five days after Tank, and within a week of his freedom, he offered Tank a job. In fact, he employed Suga, Playa, Solo and Pop. Pookie was against selling drugs, so he turned down Santiago's offer. The five drove drugs across the Texas and Mexico border. A risky job, especially for a young black male, but they were quick to jump on the distorted opportunity.

It was Tank's sixty-sixth day of freedom from captivity, and he had been doing good he thought to himself. He had saved at least a thousand dollars, and always had at least two hundred and fifty dollars in his pockets. The crew seemed to be prospering in their evil endeavors. Playa and Pop even bought two used cars for themselves. Tank felt that it would look too suspicious if he bought a car, since on paper he didn't have a source of income. However, the posse having access to three cars was a good thing, he reasoned to himself. They often talked about paying

Bluepoints posse a visit to retaliate for what they had done, but Tank still wasn't ready. He always said, "There's a time for everything, and now's our time to make money, but their time will come." The posse was anxious for revenge, but more so for blood money. You see, they knew that what they were doing was wrong, but that's what attracted them to it. The idea of rebelling against society was the reason they woke up each morning and did what they did.

CHAPTER 2

THE PLOT and PAYBACK

It was 10:30 a.m. when Tank jumped out of sleep. He had a series of dreams that were discomforting. He couldn't remember the dream exactly, but he remembered that it was displeasing. It wasn't that he was superstitious, but he often dreamed things that came to pass. He got out of bed with a bewildered look on his face, as if he had witnessed an unsolved mystery. After taking care of his personal hygiene, he put on his gang uniform. He would most likely smuggle drugs across the border that day, so he chose not to dress too flashy, so as not to receive unneeded attention to his illegal activity. Before he left home, he devoured a bowl of cereal, and called Playa, his partner in crime. Playa's telephone rang twice before he answered it. "Talk about it." It was Tank.

"What's up partner? Is you bout it today?"

Playa showed his loyalty to the command of Tank by answering, "Just lead and I'll follow."

"Come pick me up and we'll talk in person."

"Alright. Gimme a few minutes, dog."

Beep Beep. Tank heard the horn while he was watching rap videos. He looked out of the window and saw Playa's car, unoccupied. He glanced down the street and saw Playa rapping to a female in a flashy suit. Tank became angry at this sight, and with a sense of urgency, hollered, "Yo, Playa, bring your crazy self over here!"

After Playa received the girl's telephone number, he walked to his car. Tank said, "What's wrong with you? Is you stupid my nigga? We vinna blow up and look at you. You got on all of this jewelry, you don't work, and to top it off, you talking to a sixteen-year-older. You must wanna be arrested for statutory rape? Trust me nigga, you don't wanna go to prison, and I don't need to go back, but it's like you're moving backward, and is gonna get us all busted! I'm saying man, you can look clean without bringing all this attention on us, you see what I'm saying?"

Playa was a stubborn individual, but he knew that Tank was right so he whispered, "Yeah."

"What?"

"Yeah man, I heard you."

"On the real, we gonna do this correct, pay them punk nigga's back, and just live happily ever after."

There was silence in the car when Tank finally broke the ice. "Let's park the car and go over to the gambling house." The two kinsmen parked in Solo's parking space, took a shortcut, and within five minutes, they were at the gambling house. As planned, Solo, Pop and Suga were there as well, eager to carry out their distorted order (Also known as, `paying your dues`). Solo volunteered to be the bearer of the bad news. "Remember that nigga, Red?"

Tank answered, "Yeah, why?"

Solo slowly nodded his head in disgust as he said, "That nigga got cancer, man." Tank and Playa were dumbfounded by the unfortunate revelation. Tank didn't believe it, so he asked, "How do you know?"

"Me and Pop went to the flea market; that's where we saw his gal and she told us."

"She told y'all which hospital he at?"

"He's on the fourteenth floor at MD. Sanderson, she said. We should visit him."

Tank didn't even think twice when he said, "No doubt, we got to check the big homie out."

On the way to the hospital, they picked up Pookie. During the whole trip, one could sense that the posse was still in disbelief about Red's deteriorating condition. Solo rolled a joint, and lit it on Red's behalf; "This is for Red." The other five agreed to dedicate the ritual to a legend on the streets of Willowcreek. It was 1:15 p.m. when they arrived at the hospital.

When they reached room 1406, they noticed that the door was closed. Rather than barging in, Tank knocked on the door to give Red notice before they entered. When no one answered after five knocks, the posse entered. To their surprise, Red was wide-awake, staring to see who it was.

"What's up Red?"

Red recognized the young thugs and said, "What's up y'all? I thought that y'all was the nurses knocking; they be getting on my nerves." Everybody gave Red a hug, and properly greeted him. Tank was the first to ask, "How are you feeling, Homie?"

Red answered while struggling to sit up, "I've felt better man. So when did you get out of prison?"

"About two and a half months ago."

The two had spent about a year together in Huntsville prison. Similar to Tank, Red was considered a legend on the streets of Willowcreek. Red was a twenty-seven-year old thug who had previously lived in Willowcreek, but after he came out of prison, he moved to a different part of town. Red was feeling lethargic so he whispered, "You remember when we had that riot in prison?"

"Yeah man. I can't never forget that! You remember when you knocked out that punk guard? I said to myself that you is a crazy nigga when you did that."

"Yeah man, I hated that guard," Red continued. "They gave me about two months of solitary confinement for that, but it was worth it." Everyone laughed at Red's remark, trying to get him to laugh.

Tank said, "You a crazy nigga, Red."

"Me?" Red alertly responded. "Nigga, I remember when you knocked out that nigga from Georgia."

Tank recalled, "He was always talking about how Georgia niggas were fresher than Texas niggas. So I had to shut him up."

Red began to cough and spit up phlegm. "I'm sure glad that y'all came to check me out. A lot of niggas that I thought would of come and visited me ain't even called me, much less to see me."

Playa interjected, "We had to give respect where respect is due."

Solo joined in on the conversation, "Your real people will always give you respect. You still got us, your family, and your girl."

Red quickly responded, "I don't know about no girl. I ain't putting my faith in no female. She's probably laid up with another nigga as we speak. Who knows, who cares?"

Solo rebuked that idea. "Naw man, she ain't doing that."

"When I was in prison, she was doing that, so what's to stop her from doing that now?"

Just then, Playa's cellular telephone began to ring, so he told Tank to take a message for him. When he answered, the voice on the other end said, "I need y'all to make a run for me right now." Tank recognized the voice to be that of Santiago, so he said, "We can't right now, but as soon as we're free, we'll call you." Santiago answered back, noticeably irritated, "What do you mean you can't? Look, you work for me now, and I said that I need y'all to make a run for me now, not later!"

Tank, not liking to be ordered, said, "Calm down, man! We're visiting a friend in the hospital. Like I said, we'll be about another hour."

Santiago raised his voice. "I don't think you understood me. Get over here now!"

Tank could no longer hold in his words. "First of all, you don't ever order me around, and secondly, I said we'll be there in an hour!"

"Look here, you cockroach, if it wasn't for me, you would still be doing petty crimes, so I can order you."

Tank laughed. "Slow down. You don't need to talk to me like that because I'll slap you in your face."

"I am going to kill you, you small time nigger!" Santiago said as he slammed the phone down.

After Tank closed the cell phone, Red said, "Go handle your business man. Ya'll can check me out anytime."

"Don't worry about it partner." Tank said. "You remember that Colombian cat, Santiago from prison?"

"Yeah, I remember that dude."

"Yeah, that punk is talking junk in my ear, but I got something for him."

Red gasped for air before he said, "I'm just saying man, if you got to handle your business, I can understand that."

"Dog, we came to visit you, and can't nobody alive stop us from doing that."

The other five guys had no choice but to follow the decision of Tank. I suppose that they stayed at the hospital another hour just trying to get Red's mind off his affliction. As they were leaving the room, Red's girlfriend came in. If looks could kill, Red would have committed first degree murder right there in the hospital. Catina kissed Red on the lips before she asked him, "How're you doing baby?"

"I got cancer, how do you think I'm doing?"

The six thugs said their good-byes to Red and left the room.

Once on the elevator, Tank said, "Damn man, that nigga Red got a low blow! I sure hate to see that." All of them voiced their empathy for Red.

Once they were all in the car, Tank said in a vindictive voice, "Tonight's the night we carry out justice on Bluepoints posse!" He also told his comrades that they were going to war against Santiago and his friends.

"Nigga's taking us for clowns. It's time to let them know the deal." The posse knew that they would have to buy some guns if they were going to go on the offensive. Playa was the first to voice his opinion. "If we gonna go to war, we got to at least be packing."

"Word up, we gonna get some gats from the nigga Smiley," Tank agreed.

Pookie stuttered, "D-didn't that nigga get locked up?"

Pop snapped, "Look, if you scared, you don't have to do this! I rather have five real niggas, than five niggas with one fake nigga."

Pookie didn't answer back, but deep down inside, he was relieved that Pop had said that.

Solo pulled out another joint, and played his new cassette. No one said a word; there was complete silence in the car for the remainder of the ride. On arrival to Willowcreek, Tank and Playa agreed to pay Smiley a visit and inquire about his services. The other four went to the gambling house and just hung out.

When Tank and Playa arrived at Smiley's house, Tank knocked on the door. You could tell that someone was staring out of the peephole, because it got dark. Once the peephole showed light again, you could hear three bolts being unlocked. When Smiley opened up he said, "What up fools? Y'all come in."

Tank said, "What's up man?" Playa looked at the locks on the door and said, "It looks like you got some enemies, my nigga."

"We all got enemies. Sometimes it's your best friend, you feel me cuz?" Smiley responded.

"True that," Tank said, wanting to proceed with business, because Smiley's paranoia was giving him the creeps. Smiley also wanted to deal with business so he said, "So what brings y'all here?"

Tank elected himself the spokesman on the posse's behalf. "We want to buy a few burners."

Smiley looked into Tank and Playa's eyes. "This is y'all lucky day, because I have a few."

"What kind do you got?"

Smiley lit a cigarette before answering. "If you get specific, then I'll get specific."

Tank and Playa consulted each other before Tank said, "We want five nine millimeters and a sawed-off shotgun." Smiley pondered to himself, then said, "That'll be seven hundred."

Tank thought that that was a steep price. "Seven hundred! Some cats around the way said five fifty for the same thing."

Smiley got defensive at that. "They probably was gonna sell y'all some gats that got bodies on them. You can whistle with my gats they're so clean."

"Look, the lowest I can go is six hundred and fifty." Tank, who played poker from time to time, knew how to call the other guy's bluff. "Can't you sell them to us for six hundred?"

Smiley wasn't that smart, but he knew that he had just got hustled. "I don't have them right now, but if you come back at 5:00, they'll be ready."

Tank looked at his watch and agreed that they would be there precisely.

The two had to wait at least ten more seconds for Smiley to unlock the door and let them out. Tank said, "Man, I don't know about that nigga, Smiley."

"I know. I think that nigga's smoking that cocaine." Playa agreed.

"Boy look here, I kind of got nervous being in his house. Were you?" Tank asked, wiping sweat off his forehead.

"Man I was busting cold sweats, I was so nervous!"

In five minutes, the two were at the gambling house with the other rogues. Tank asked, "Where is that nigga Pookie?" Pop hit his heart with his fist and said, "Man, Pookie ain't got no heart. He ran home like a little girl. I don't even know why he's a part of our crew."

Suga followed, "For real, dog, that nigga do be acting shady at times."

Playa said, "That nigga ain't about nothing. He lived in every part of Houston. I know he wouldn't go to war for Willowcreek."

Solo also voted to revoke Pookie's membership into the posse by adding, "Yeah man, he just makes a nigga laugh, but truly, I don't trust him."

Tank confirmed the veto of Pookie's membership. "Oh yeah, I know that he isn't deep into the game, but he's still good people. But on the real, he ain't officially down for the cause."

As easy as that, Pookie was alienated from being a member of the crew. They all agreed that he was a cool person to hang around with, but when it came to criminal activities, he was a definite outcast. Tank also told the others of his meeting with Smiley, and the exact price of the merchandise.

By this time it was 2:45, so for the remainder of the afternoon, the gang gambled and eagerly waited for 5:00 to come around. At 4:50, the posse left the gambling house and went to Solo's apartment. Once they arrived, Pop said, "I hope y'all niggas is ready, cause we're about to do this."

They arrived at Smiley's a quarter after the hour. Tank said to Playa, "Let's go get our tools from this schizophrenic nigga." Smiley seemed to be anticipating them, because this time he answered the door quickly. He scolded them for their tardiness. "Damn man, it's 5:20. Y'all was suppose to be here twenty minutes ago. I have a tight schedule. Do y'all got the money?"

Tank and Playa fully entered the house when Playa said, "We're sorry man. We had to get the money, and you wouldn't want to know how we got it."

Smiley, still noticeably irritated, said, "You're right. I don't want to know. I just want to take care of business. Y'all got the money are what?"

"You show us the guns and we'll give you the money." Smiley bristled at Tank's remark. "Lookit here, dogs, I'm a professional at this. I'm going to keep my end of the deal. I just want to know if y'all did, you feel me?"

Tank was satisfied with that so he gave Smiley the money.

He counted it before he went into the room, and returned with a book bag. "Here it is, five nines and a sawed-off. Y'all didn't ask for no clips, but I supplied 'em."

Tank and Playa examined the guns before Tank said, "For real, man, this is what I'm talking about."

Before the two left Smiley's apartment, Tank reassured him that he was satisfied, and in the future they would continue to do business with him.

Tank distributed the guns to everyone, as if he was giving away government cheese. Before they realized it, they were in Bluepoints' territory. Solo drove until he saw three of the rival gang members. Tank asked him, "Is that joint rolled up?" Solo answered, "Yeah."

"Alright, let's hurry up and smoke this, then pay these nigga's back."

After they finished the reefer, they were more anxious than before to carry out revenge.

Solo drove in front of the gangsters, and before they could react, the Willowcreek members were out of the car with drawn guns. They forced the three lonely gang members into the car with them. Tank said to Solo, "Let's get out of here!" As expected, Pop was the most aggressive towards the three. He was busy gun-butting all of the adversaries. Playa said, "Pop, take it easy! These niggas is bleeding all over the place!"

Pop answered back, "Chill out nigga! Why you hollering out my name?"

Solo glanced back and noticed the blood. "Now, nigga, you chill out. Don't be getting my car dirty with these niggas' blood!"

Suga was choking the biggest one while searching through his pocket, "Man, you ain't got no money. I ought to cap you!"

There was complete chaos in the car for a moment. The victims were screaming at the top of their lungs, and the perpetrators were quite noisy themselves. Tank decided to take control of the situation. "Y'all nigga's shut up before we kill y'all! Hurry up and take off all of your clothes!" At first, they tried to object, but their defiance brought on more beatings from their adversaries, so eventually they stripped. After their clothes were off, Tank held a spray paint bottle and gave a speech. "Look, y'all is brothers so we're gonna spare your lives, but because your crew jacked us. We got to pay y'all back."

It was as if Solo knew the game plan because he drove directly to the mall where all this trouble had started and said, "Let's dump these fools." They spray-painted "Willowcreek" on their chests, and pistol-whipped them before they threw them out of the car.

"Dog, they almost pissed on themselves they were so scared!" Pop said, trying to control his laughter. Playa found it hilarious also. "Them niggas thought we were gonna kill them. Did you see how fast they ran when we let them go?"

Solo said in a serious voice as he saw the blood on his car seat, "Hey, Pop you be getting out of control. I hope you know you got to clean up this blood!"

"Man, why you acting like a little girl? I can barely see any blood!" Pop shot back.

Suga sided with Pop: "You can't be worried about no blood. Them niggas started it, so what's the problem?"

"Ain't nobody talking to you, nigga," Solo said as he glanced at Suga.

Tank intervened as usual. "We was easy on them, man. We could have did anything to them fools and wouldn't nobody know a thing. Actually, we should have made them niggas examples, but the black on black crime is whack. However, if it makes you feel better, we'll all help you to clean up, because one for all and all for one. But first we're gonna pay them Colombians a visit."

"How are we gonna know where to find them?" Solo asked Tank.

"Go to Los Fiesta. I know that he's there," Tank answered. Suga said, "I thought you were through dealing with him?" Tank had a menacing look on his face when he said, "We're gonna shoot their club up, and show him that we ain't no joke."

"Man, we're gonna have to off them, are else they'll come back for us. Them Colombians are crazy!" Solo said in a concerned voice.

Pop liked the idea and said, "Yeah dog, let's get them! We got to show them that niggas don't mess around."

With apprehension in his voice, Solo said, "What if they ain't there? What are we gonna do?"

Tank said in a reassuring voice, "They gonna be there. Hey Playa, is you down are what?"

"I'm down for what ever."

So it was settled. Willowcreek was going to attack their Hispanic adversaries. Los Fiesta was about a thirty-minute drive from Bluepoints mall. Solo lit another joint and played some gangster hip-hop music. The car was unusually quiet for the whole ride. The only thing that could be heard was the loud music. Each member of the posse seemed to be miles away in deep meditation. It was as if they knew that this was a major move that would have destructive consequences. They all knew that Santiago and his crew were the most deadly gangsters they had ever come across, but Tank was determined to punish Santiago for his remarks.

Being confined in prison had made Tank pro-black, so when Santiago called him a black nigger, it was as if he had invited Tank to a gunfight. To make matters worst, Santiago had embarrassed him in front of his street soldiers. This was definitely going to be a critical move for the posse, and the strange thing about it was that they all were aware of that. The closer they got to the club, the tenser the atmosphere in the car became.

When they were two blocks away from the club, Pop broke the silence by suggesting that they buy some beer so that they would loosen up. After they got the beer, they waited in the car outside of the club to spot Santiago, or anyone who had the misfortune to be with him on that particular day. By this time it was 6:30 p.m., and they figured Santiago and his friends wouldn't be coming out of the club anytime soon. Fifteen minutes later, they finished all of the beer and smoked another joint. The beer did the job, because they were in an even more violent mood than before, and the weed was like the icing on the cake. The gangsters patiently waited another fifteen minutes, but grew weary from hearing the same songs play again. Tank finally said, "Yo man, forget this! Let's go in there and ransack the place!" The other members, tipsy and impatient, agreed entirely.

Tank ordered the strategy for the battle. "Eh, Solo, you stay in the car and wait for us. Suga and Pop, y'all wait outside and be look out. I don't care if the president shows up, don't let him come in. Me and Playa is gonna go in and let off some shots. Suga and Pop, y'all be listening, because if we need y'all we're gonna holler. Y'all be listening real good, because I got a feeling that these fools is gonna be packing. Everybody understand?" They all agreed to their assigned positions.

Santiago was in Los Fiesta as Tank had predicted. He was

sitting at his normal table. Two street soldiers and four half-dressed young ladies accompanied him. Each had a plate of food, and a drink in front of them. Santiago was drunk with his arms around two of the ladies' shoulders, and was unaware that the two thugs had entered the club. At that instance, Playa noticed Santiago and pointed towards the table. What followed was a flurry of gunshots let off by the two thugs. They caught their adversaries unaware, as they had hoped to. As a result, there was total pandemonium in the club, screaming, running and ducking all over. Tank and Playa emptied their guns in the direction of Santiago and his company at the table. They weren't sure if they hit anyone, but after their guns were empty, the two exited the restaurant and hopped into the car. Everything took place in less than twenty seconds.

Everyone in the car was uptight, and knew more than likely there would be some form of retaliation. Solo took the highway straight back to Willowcreek. Cautious enough not to be pulled over by a trooper, yet he was still driving faster than the law allowed.

Once they made it back to Willowcreek, they all decided to lay low that night, just in case Santiago decided to strike back right away. It was an anxious moment, so they all went to Playa and Suga's house to play video games.

About ten seconds after the gunshots had ceased and Santiago realized that the gunmen had dispersed, he got up from under the table. He felt a sharp pain in his left shoulder. When he examined it, he saw that he had been hit by one of the bullets. One of his colleagues got up after him and brushed himself off too to see if he too was hit. Around that time, everyone was getting up from the ground, obviously shaken up by the two gunmen's action. Santiago and his colleague looked on the ground and saw that their five friends were lying there, motionless in a pool of blood. This infuriated the two Colombians, especially Santiago, because he had recognized the two gunmen. They tried to revive the corpses, but to no avail. All five of them died instantly; they didn't even know what hit them. Santiago said some bad words in his native tongue, and vowed to avenge the deaths of his friends. Although his colleague wasn't shot, he agreed to retaliate. To prove his sincerity to the cause, he picked up a broken piece of bottle off the floor and stuck himself in the shoulder with it so that, although it was self-inflicted, he himself had suffered bodily injury from this attack. I guess it is appropriate to say that it was written in blood that Santiago and his boys were going to war against Tank and his boys.

When the five young hoodlums got to Playa and Suga's house, Grandma was reading her Bible as usual. She looked up and saw the five young adolescents. Before she began her lecture, she took off her eyeglasses and took a sip of ice water. "I'm glad that y'all are alright. I had a bad feeling all day."

"What kind of bad feeling, Mama?" Tank asked her, still paranoid from the earlier event. Before she answered, Playa, sensing a speech, said, "We're alright, Mama. We just came to play some video games, but you and Tank can discuss your bad feeling."

While the other four walked towards the room, Grandma said, "I can only pray for you boys, but God's spirit doesn't strive with man always; remember what I say."

When they reached the room, Playa closed the door behind them, and Grandma proceeded, "I pray for those boys, but I know God is calling you, so you have to respond. But the bad feeling that I had was as a result of a vision I had." Before Grandma could continue, Tank, who was listening intently, asked, "What was the vision, Mama?"

Grandma, liking the fact that Tank was paying such attention, continued. "I was at a cemetery and a body ascended from a grave. When I saw this, I was frightened, but the corpse told me to listen to him because I have to relay this message to the kids. I asked him which kids, and he said all of the kids. I'm almost certain that the kids he was referring to was you children."

"What did he tell you to tell the kids?"

"Just what I told the other boys. God doesn't strive with man always."

"What that means, Mama?"

"Everyday that you wake up, God is with you. In fact, throughout the day, God gives us blessings. That simply means that one day you'll find yourself receiving no more blessings. You'll have to face judgement without Jesus as your advocate."

Tank took in a deep breath. "That's deep, Mama. So what would I have to do to make Jesus my advocate?"

Grandma held onto his hands. "All you have to do is ask Jesus into your heart by faith, and believe that he has the power to forgive your sins. Don't worry about changing yourself, because he said to come as you are."

Tank wanted to accept the offer but he resisted. "I would, Mama, but I don't want to be a hypocrite, because I know that I wouldn't fully commit myself."

Grandma understood his apprehension and said, "Alright, Baby, but remember what I said. God's spirit doesn't strive with man always. You can be here today and gone tomorrow, and if you don't have God then hell awaits you."

Before he went to the room with the rest of the fellows, Tank gave Grandma a hug and said, "You're a real virtuous woman." Grandma gave him a kiss on the cheek and concluded her talk by saying, "I'll keep you in my prayer, because I know that God is calling you for a specific reason."

CHAPTER 3

RETALIATION and THE HEIST

Santiago managed to round up three more of his friends, which made five of them heavily armed. Santiago knew where the posse lived, so he and his comrades drove to Willowcreek and staked out the area. He was a quick-tempered Colombian with all kinds of connections. Initially, he wasn't going to worry about the argument, but after the shooting, he had no choice but to retaliate.

Once in the bedroom, Tank told the other four that they had to come up with a plan to get some money. They all did petty crime, but Santiago had helped to raise their illegal ambition to a new level. So now that they were in war against Santiago, they could forget about going back to him for employment. The main thing that bugged Tank was the fact that he had tasted a bit of the fast life, and now he and his soldiers were forced to start all over. "Turn that stupid game off. Let's plan our next move," he ordered Playa.

Pop said, "Hey dog, we still control the park, so we ain't got nothing to worry about."

Tank squinted his eyes in Pop's direction as if he had made a rude remark. "Nigga, we only be making chump change in the park. We in war, so we need some real money."

"So what should we do?" Pop asked.

Tank walked into the middle of the gang. "I been watching that bank on Belleville Road. They only got one security guard, and he looks like he should be retired, living in Miami."

"Damn man, that's a big job there! Do you think we can pull it off?" Suga blurted out.

Tank put his fingers up to his lips. "Keep your voice down nigga. But on the real, I been watching it, and I know that we can pull it off with ease."

Solo got up and stared out of the window. "So do they got a lot of money in there?"

"I don't know exactly how much they got, but I know that we'll get more than we can make in the park. Every Monday morning, an armored truck picks up a chunk of money from there."

Playa clutched his gun and said, "Dog, I'm down. All I need is a stocking and just say the word and I will be there." Tank looked at the other three. "What about y'all? Is y'all down with that?" They all agreed.

Before Tank concluded the conversation, he made sure that the door was shut and then he whispered, "I don't know if we hit Santiago. I guess we'll see that on the news later on, so we need to lay low for now. And don't be bragging about nothing. If they wasn't there, then they don't need to know." The posse agreed that they would be scarce, and took an oath of silence.

At that same time, Santiago and his crew were driving to the gang's hangout. They planned on seeing Tank and his posse there, and without any discussion, committing a drive-by shooting. They waited in the car about thirty minutes before they saw Pookie. Santiago exited the car and called Pookie to him. Pookie came to the car, totally oblivious to the fight between Willowcreek and Santiago. Although Santiago knew that Pookie knew the gang, he knew that Pookie wasn't involved with the shooting. Santiago asked him, "Do you know where Tank is?"

"Naw, man, I just came from work."

Santiago became angry and ordered Pookie inside of the car. The driver pulled off as soon as Pookie entered. Santiago said, "Look I need to talk to Tank about some unfinished business we have together. I know that you know where he is, so just let me know and there'll be no problems."

Pookie felt threatened but he still said, "I don't know where he is. I don't see that nigga every day."

Santiago reached into his pocket. "Here's my number. If you see him, just give me a call; it's important that I talk to him. I'm even willing to give you a thousand dollars if you do that." After everything was said, the driver made an abrupt stop and Santiago gave Pookie permission to leave the car. Pookie now knew that Tank had a price on his head, but he relentlessly hung on to the phone-number. Even though Tank was his friend, a thousand dollars was a tempting offer for a brother receiving minimum wage.

While Pookie was walking home, he was weighing the pros and cons of Santiago's offer. He reasoned to himself, "I can't roll on Tank, that's my nigga, but I could use a thousand dollars. I have to find out what happened with them today." He knew that they were at Playa's house, so he stopped there before he went home.

Suga answered and said, "What's up man? Ain't your mama gonna be bugging out because you're out so late?"

"Why you trippin man? Are you gonna let me inside are

what?" Pookie asked. As he walked towards the bedroom, Grandma said, "The spirit of GOD doesn't strive with man always."

Pookie politely said to her, "I know, Mam."

The rest of the gang was in the room, so Pookie said, "What's up y'all? What y'all nigga's did today? Did y'all get them Colombians?"

Playa quickly asked, "Why you worried nigga?"

Tank intervened and said, "Naw man, they ain't worth it. Why you asking?"

"I was just wondering if y'all got them punk niggas."

Pop vindictivaly said, "Why you calling them punk nigga's, and you was scared to bust at them!"

Pookie answered, "You know I ain't a gangster like y'all niggas."

Pop said, "You ain't about nothing, nigga. I don't even know why you be coming around, fool!"

Tank sensed the animosity. "Naw, man, Pookie's alright."

That simple statement made it all the more hard for Pookie to betray Tank for thirty pieces of silver, but not impossible. Pookie hung around another five minutes before he made his way home. He thought to himself, They don't even know that I have their destiny in my hands. He didn't call Santiago that night, but he entertained the thought in his mind.

One by one the others all went home and agreed to contact each other the following day.

At 7:30 a.m., Tank arose out of bed and cleaned himself up. When he came back into the room, he saw Tameka sleeping in the bed, looking so peaceful and serene. The two had had a brief relationship before he went to prison. It was not a monogamous relationship; in fact, she was supposedly in love with another guy. Tameka's boyfriend was at the University of Florida on a basketball scholarship, so from time to time, she would seek companionship from a gangster. Tank had his own bachelor apartment, so this made him an eligible lover.

At 8:15 a.m., Tank woke up Tameka and told her that it was time for her to go home. She was furious. "What time is it? You wake me up this early to tell me to go home? You wasn't saying that last night. I'm a stop messing with you, because all you want from me is sex!"

Tank looked at her as if she was speaking a different language. "Of course that's all I want from you. You got a man so what do you expect?"

This got her irate. She got up, went into the bathroom for a few minutes, came back out dressed, and while she was leaving she said, "You make me sick, Frank. Don't ever call me." While she was shutting the door, Tank shouted, "Whatever." He knew that she was sensitive, but she would be back, no matter what. He knew that he held a special place in her heart and technically, he was right.

He turned on the news and saw everything from the Dow-Jones, gossip about celebrities, the weather, and then finally he heard about the shooting. The reporter said, "Last night around 8:00 p.m., two black suspects entered Los Fiesta for no apparent reason but to kill. Six people were shot, five of them died on the scene, and one received non- life threatening wounds. When police asked the witnesses the descriptions of the assailants, no one could remember. Anyone with information about this shooting is urged to call 411- tips. Remember that your identity will remain anonymous."

Within ten seconds, the report was over. Although Tank was glad that the report was concise, he was not ignorant to the fact that if it had been a police officer who was killed, more effort would have been put into the report. He called all of the members to let them know that the police did not suspect them, but they should still be on the cautious side.

Uncharacteristically, Tank stayed in the entire morning, but by 1 p.m., he was eager to go outside. Therefore, he took the shortcut to Playa's house. When he arrived, Playa and Suga were sitting on the porch, smoking. Tank joined them before they went inside. They were playing some music when the knob on the door began to move. Tank noticed it and jumped up in a defensive position. Playa said, "Relax, Homie, that's only Mama coming from church."

"It looks like Santiago has you nervous," Suga smiled. Tank became defensive. "Y'all must think that this is a game. We shot up Santiago, therefore that means war."

Just then, Grandma came into the house singing a hymn. "How y'all doing boys? I wish y'all came to church this morning; it was good. Later there is a youth service with all kind of activities for y'alls age group. Y'all should come." "Mama, you know that if we go, all eyes will be on us," Playa said, declining the invitation.

Grandma answered, "If they're staring at y'all it's only because they were once like you."

In order to avoid a lecture, the boys told grandma that they would consider going, but that was an easy way of ending the argument.

At 1:30 p.m., Playa called Solo at home. He asked Solo if he had seen the news. Solo told him that he had not, because he was busy cleaning up the house. Playa cut the conversation short by saying, "We'll be over there a little later, so just wait around for us."

After that, he called Pop to see what he was doing. When Pop answered the telephone, he already sounded half-drunk. Pop told Playa that he had to take care of some business for a couple of hours, so in the meanwhile, he would continue to drink. Playa asked Pop what he was planning on doing, but Pop declined on telling him. He left it at that, but before he hung up, he told Pop to be careful with whatever he was going to do.

A little after 2:00, Pookie jumped out of bed and looked at his clock. When he realized that it was minutes after 2:00, he shouted, "Damn!" because he was supposed to be at work. Therefore, he called his boss to give him an excuse, but his boss was in no mood to hear any of Pookie's lame excuses.

Pookie became defensive and without thinking of the consequences, he cursed out his boss and quit his job. At that instance, Pookie was unemployed and more susceptible to betraying the gang.

Tank, Playa, and Suga finally got bored of playing video games, so they went to the basketball court. The court was connected to the drug dealers' paradise, so if being scarce was their intention, they certainly were not fulfilling it. Tank and Playa were playing a basketball game when Suga saw Santiago and his friends in the area, talking with the locals. He quickly broke up the game and pointed Santiago out to his partners. While wiping the sweat off his body, Tank said, "Dog, we got to go back home and think this thang through."

In a disgusted voice Playa added, "He must of put a price on our head."

Suga asked, "So what are we gonna do?"

Tank said, "The first thang we gonna do is go to Solo's house, and then call Pop over there, and we'll take it from there."

Solo was outside, washing his car, when they arrived. In an urgent voice, Tank said, "Hey yo, forget the car. Let's go inside and talk!"

When they went in, Playa called Pop and told him that it was important for him to come to Solo's house. Within five minutes, Pop was knocking at the door. Once everyone was situated, Tank stood in front of them and said, "We got a big problem. Santiago and his boys are in the park, looking for us." Solo and Pop were surprised to hear that. Tank continued, "I know that we were supposed to hit the bank next week, but plans have changed. Tomorrow's the day." Solo said, "Damn, man, I knew we shouldn't have got involved with them Colombians!"

Pop answered, "Man, forget them! I say we go outside right now and start blasting on them clowns."

Tank dismissed that. "And then do what? Our faces will be all on the news, and we'll be in a worser predicament. We'll do as I said; tomorrow we'll hit the bank and then we can finish off Santiago."

The tone was now set. The posse agreed to rob the bank early the next morning before the Brink's truck took away the currency. Tank originally had planned to get his crew familiar with their parts in the robbery, but due to circumstances, they would have to be spontaneous. The plan was that before 10:00 a.m., the crew had to take the money, because the money would be deposited by then. It seemed like a foolproof crime, but then again, there are no such crimes in existence.

In the middle of scheming, Roketta came out of the bedroom and overheard them discussing the robbery. Without thinking, she said, "Y'all thinking about robbing a bank? Kenneth, you better not get involved, or do you want to go to prison like your boy, Tank?"

In a fury, Solo said, "Shut up girl! You don't know what you're talking about. Get out of here and give us some privacy." Since she was stubborn, Roketta answered back, "This is my place. I go to any room that I want to. Can't you or anyone else make me leave!"

Solo was both embarrassed as well as mad, and was going to physically remove Roketta from the room, but Tank told him that she was right; they should leave instead. Solo followed them to further discuss the robbery.

The posse went to Tank's apartment knowing that they would receive no interruptions there. Once inside, Tank resumed where he had left off. "Now this is how it's going to go down. We're going to steal a van tonight, and by 8:00 a.m., we're going to be there. It opens at 9:00, but all of the employees are there by 8:30, so we'll be there slightly ahead of them. The manager drives a red mustang, and when he gets there, it all begins. We can't be in there any longer than four minutes. I don't care if you see a million dollars in cash, as soon as four minutes passes, we're out of there. Solo, you'll drive, because you're the most experienced driver out of us all. Suga, you'll make sure the other employees don't try anything heroic, but don't shoot unless it's totally necessary.

"Me, Playa, and Pop will be the clean-up men. We'll get the manager to crack the safe, and for four minutes, we'll be picking money off a tree. We have to steal a car tonight, and leave it at Southline Mall. Solo, before we go to the bank, you're going to park your car at Southline Mall, take the other car, and after we hit the bank, we'll drive to the mall and switch cars. After that, we'll drive back to my crib and split the money five ways. Is that clear y'all?" Everyone agreed but Playa. He asked, "So what about masks?"

Tank said, "Oh yeah, we're going to wear stockings over our faces." Then Playa agreed.

They all agreed that this would be a simple move if everyone fulfilled his part. Solo rolled a fat joint and said, "This is for a smooth get-away tomorrow." Although there was a risk in carrying out a robbery, the consequences were lighter than that of shooting up Santiago and his gang. They knew that they would eventually have to deal with Santiago because they were already feeling too confined.

After everyone left, Tank took a little nap. At 5:00 p.m., he was awakened by the telephone. When he answered it, Tameka asked, "What you doing, Frank?"

"Nothing. I'm just lounging."

"Do you know that you hurt my feelings this morning? Is that all I am to you, just sex?"

"I mean, I wasn't trying to hurt your feelings, but it's just that you already have a man. So what else is our relationship?"

"Frank, you know that I love you, and I would do anything for you. The reason why your remark hurt me so much is because I'd like to think that we have something more than just sex," she desperately said.

"I care for you a lot, too, Tameka, but I can't put myself out on a limb, especially seeing that you already have a man. I mean, what happens when he comes back in town? That ain't fair, to him nor to me."

Tears began to roll down Tameka's brown eyes. "I don't know Frank; I'm so confused. I mean, you know that I love you, but I also have strong feelings for Derek. I don't know what to do. What do you think I should do Frank?"

"I ain't trying to be rude, but I'm not a counselor. But if you really care for both of us like you claim, you'll go with your heart, because right now you aren't being fair to either of us."

"Can I come over and see you? I just want to be in your strong arms right now."

"Sure. I'm not stopping you, but I'm letting you know that tomorrow morning I have to leave early."

Immediately after Tank hung the telephone up, it rang again. Solo sounded sad. "I got some bad news, dog, Catina just called me, and told me that Red passed away." One could sense the hurt that Tank felt. "Damn, man, we just saw that nigga a couple days ago. I ain't even get to see him again. Do she know where his funeral is going to be at, and when it's gonna be?"

Solo said, "She never told me about it, but I'll ask her when it's easier for her to talk about it." This news put a bad feeling in Tank's heart, but he tried to rationalize it by saying, "At least he's in a better place."

At 6:15 p.m., Tank's doorbell rang. When he looked through the peephole, he saw Tameka wearing a leather trench coat. When she entered, before Tank could close the door, she gave him a passionate kiss. He was feeling down, but Tameka's slightest touch still stimulated him. While they were still kissing, she slid off her coat, which enticed Tank even more. She was wearing a tiny lingerie which was transparent. She made her way to the bed and invited Tank to follow her. In many aspects, Tank was a born leader, but when it came to sex, he was persuaded easily. He followed her, and the rest can be explained in a sex education class.

After Tank climaxed, he said, "I just found out that one of my homies died."

Tameka embraced him. "I'm sorry to hear that, Baby. Who was it?"

"It was a cool brother that I met way back in the days. However, when I went to prison, him and me became tight. Who would of thought that Red would lose his life to cancer? He was a real soldier."

"Don't worry, I'll be here for you." Tameka said

They talked for a few more minutes when the doorbell rang with a buzzing sound that seemed to echo and startled them both. "Are you expecting someone, Frank?"

He ignored the question, and quietly walked over to the door. When he saw that it was Pookie, he went back to bed. "Who was that at the door?" Tameka asked him suspiciously.

"It's Pookie, not that it's any of your business."

She held her peace, realizing that he was obviously upset over the demise of his friend.

Pookie heard Tank at the door, and when he didn't answer, he left. That was when Pookie made a conscious decision to betray the gang. He thought to himself, "I need the money, plus them niggas be acting like they don't know me." At that moment, the fate of the posse was sealed. It was the beginning of the end.

At around 7:30 p.m., the crew called Tank, ready to carry out Phase one of the heist, the stealing of a car. He got dressed and went to Solo's house to meet up with them.

Everyone was there, so as soon as Tank arrived, they just drove off in search of a vehicle. It didn't take them long to spot one. Suga went into the night, and within 30 seconds, he was driving away. He drove straight to the mall with the rest of them following in Solo's car.

The night went by easier than any of them had expected, so once back into the hood, they reviewed the roles that they would each carry out in the robbery. When Tank felt that everyone knew their role with perfect precision, he told them to go home and sleep, because they all had to wake up bright and early the following morning.

When Tank reached home, Tameka was in the kitchen eating some spaghetti. She seemed happy to see him. "Are you hungry Baby? Would you like some spaghetti?" Without second thoughts he answered, "Yes I'm starving like Marvin."

"All right, Baby, just make yourself comfortable at the table, and I'll take care of everything." She came back with a plate of spaghetti and a glass of red wine.

"What's this for?" he asked in a perplexed tone. She just slid her finger over his lips and motioned for him to eat up.

After he finished eating, she seductively played with him, and before you knew it, they were inseparable. Tank knew that he had to be up and alert the following morning, so he took a shower and was in bed by eleven. Of course, Tameka reserved a spot for herself next to him.

Tank's alarm clock broke the silence that reigned in his room. He eagerly anticipated this heist to be simple, but rewarding.

The first thing he did was to call his comrades to make sure they all were awake.

At 7:55 a.m., they went to the mall to retrieve the car they had boosted. By 8:10, they were outside waiting to see the red mustang, which was to be occupied by the manager.

It happened like clockwork. At 8:30, the red mustang drove into the parking lot, totally oblivious to the stolen car. The four thugs put on their masks, and met the manager and an employee at the door. He reluctantly let them into the bank, and locked the door after.

The manager begged for his life as he opened the safe. When he opened it, the hoodlums were dumbfounded to see the large pile of money. They each had two garbage bags, but after seeing the large sum of money, they regretted not having more. Three minutes after arrival, they had no more room to stuff the money, so they filled their pockets.

Once in the get-away car they shouted out jubilantly, as if their favorite team had won the championship on the last second of the game. On their way home, they stopped at the store, and purchased five bottles of the finest champagne money could buy.

When they had divided the money between themselves, they each received $7,250. They had got off with nearly $40,000, and left behind about that much, because of lack of space. They were all ecstatic, but the love of money only breeds greed, hatred and strife. They agreed on going out later.

CHAPTER 4

INDECENT PROPOSAL

By 11:58 a.m., everyone involved in the heist went his separate way. Tank was so excited that he told Tameka to put on some clothes because he had a surprise for her. She was honored that Tank would bring her out into the town and sport her as a boyfriend would his girlfriend. At 12:30 p.m., they went on their mid-day rendezvous together. Tank decided to rent a car. Although he did not own a credit card, he flashed $500 to the manager, and as quick as that, he was on his way. As he drove away, he posed in the black Sedan Deville. By 1:45 p.m., they reached Astroworld.

At that same time, Solo and Roketta were on their way to lunch. It wasn't lunch at Mc Donald's or Burger King as was the norm, but instead it was an exquisite restaurant in an expensive part of town. Although she didn't condone the fact that Solo had robbed a bank, Roketta was too flattered to give him a hard time. After lunch, they both bought enough clothes to last a few weeks.

At that exact time, Playa and Suga were at the flea market buying clothes while talking to girls. They met a set of twins that drew all of the guys' attention. The twins ignored all of the other guys, but Playa and Suga seemed to appeal to the sisters, since they were toting several shopping bags filled with clothes. They even treated the glamorous girls to lunch at the cafeteria. The girls were so comfortable with the two thugs, they let them drive them home. One could tell that the twins were interested in the cousins. One, because they let them drive them home, and two, because the girls invited them to their birthday party which was to be held the following Saturday night. Playa and Suga agreed to come by and treat the girls extra special on their twentieth anniversary to life.

At the same time, Pop was testing his luck at the horse track. He was making big shot bets. Hell, he even sat in the seating section with all of the big-shot gamblers. He had a thousand dollars and his nine-millimeter on cock. He ultimately lost all of his bets, but he managed to conceal two hundred and fifty dollars in his socks. After the last race, he decided to exit along with the hundreds of disappointed gamblers. When he was walking to his car, he glanced to his left and sighted Santiago and two more Colombians. Pop's first impulse was to sneak up on the three and do away with his enemies. However, after further thought, he realized that if he did that, he might as well walk himself to prison and ask to be executed. So instead, he got into his car and drove away.

By 5:30 p.m., Tameka and Tank had had as much fun as one is allowed to have in one day. Tank decided to drop her off home and spend the remainder of his day with his pals. Once in Willowcreek, Tank stopped at Playa's house, to consult with his confidant. Once in Playa's room, he realized that the entire posse was there and waiting for their commander and chief. Pop filled in Tank on the sighting of Santiago at the racetrack, and Playa informed him of the upcoming party.

They decided to conclude the day by going to a popular

club that was located on the other side of town. One would have easily mistaken the five thugs to be the hosts of the party. Solo and Playa were naturally talking to every girl insight. Tank, Pop, and Suga talked and danced with a fair share of girls. By the end of the party, five girls were willing to take the party to a private location. Tank offered his apartment to be the sight of the after-bash to a good day. Therefore the ten delinquents went to Tank's apartment and did whatever they did.

The door seemed to shake with each knock. After six of them, Tank finally jumped out of bed. When he finally realized that the sound effects were not a part of his dream, he looked to see who it was. By this time, everyone inside of the house was awake. When he opened the door, he only had on his boxing shorts. So Tameka said, "It must have been a long night last night. It's already a quarter to twelve and you're still in bed. Why are you being so rude? Can't I come in?"

At first, Tank was going to make up an excuse to keep her from entering, but then he said he had nothing to hide. As soon as she entered, she saw a group of girls scrambling towards their clothes. She gave Tank a dirty look and mumbled, "You're a dog!" Although she did not cause a scene, that was a sign of things to follow that day.

After Tameka left, Tank told Solo to bring the other girls home. Five p.m. was the time the gang decided to meet up again.

Prison seemed to have done Tank more harm than good, because in the three years he had been there, he made a number of connections. One such connection was a forty-year-old drug underlord, called Tyrone. He had taken a liking to the way Tank carried himself in prison, so he took him under his wing. He was serving a twelve-year bid for involuntary manslaughter. In prison, Tyrone controlled the drugs and cigarettes. With all of this control, he was feared more than the correctional officers were. His drug operation was even larger than Santiago's. The only reason Tank did not deal with Tyrone was that he had a reputation of falling out with his partners. Moreover, woe to whomever the partner was, because they were either mysteriously murdered or for no apparent reason, they supposively committed suicide.

Drastic times call for drastic measures. So Tank overlooked Tyrone's reputation and gave him a call. Tyrone gave Tank his address so they could talk business in person. Tank was desperate, so he quickly went to the house. He was shocked to see that it was in an affluent upper-class neighborhood. Once inside, Tank realized that the ex-con was as lavish on the streets as he was in prison. Tank was impressed, but he chose to conceal his amazement. "This a nice place you got here, Tyrone." While fixing a glass of liquor, Tyrone answered, "Yeah, it's alright. Would you like a shot of gin?"

"Yeah, ain't nothing wrong with one drink, big dog." Tyrone asked, "So what brings you to this part of town little man?"

Tank straightened his shirt. " I need some advice. I ran into some money and I would like to invest it before I squander it."

Tyrone took a large sip of the liquor, "What kind of money are you talking about?"

Tank was careful how he answered. "I have a little change."

Tyrone grinned and said, "What, are you robbing banks now?"

"Naw I just got a small loan from my people."

Tyrone took another drink before he said, "I don't know exactly how much money you're talking about, but one of my man's went to jail. He was running this apartment complex for me, and he made a good twenty thousand a week. Now here's the deal, I get five thousand a week; in return, I give protection and supply all of the goods."

Tank took a short pause before he answered. "Let me talk to

my people and I'll get back to you this evening." Before he left, Tyrone gave him a tour of the one and a half-acre estate.

Tank pondered the illegal proposition the whole ride home. Yes it was fast and involved large amounts of money, but when one stepped to the board with Tyrone, one was playing for keeps. For Tank, it took a thirty-minute car ride to validate the decision to play the game with Tyrone. When he got home, the first thing he did was to call Playa. He answered, "Who this?"

"Hey yo, this is me. Where you at, cuz?"

Playa giggled, "I'm at my girl's house."

Tank sounded bewildered. "Nigga you don't got no girlfriend. Which girl is you talking about?"

"Tammy, nigga."

"Man you just left a female and you're already with another one? Man, tell Tammy you got to take care of some business, and shoot over here right quick."

When Playa got off the telephone, he did just so. He reached Tank's house around ten minutes later. When Playa entered, Tank grabbed him by the shoulder and said, "We're gonna get paid, Homeboy! I know this man that offered us a fool-proof job."

"You sure he ain't like Santiago?" Playa said skeptically.

"Man, business with Santiago was good but we just had a misunderstanding. But this job is less risky, and it deals with more money. You should know that if I say it's alright, then it's alright."

Those few lines persuaded Playa enough to make him ask, "Alright Homie, then what are we gonna have to do, and what the pay looks like?"

The two eventually called Tyrone, and made an appointment to meet with him. He told them to come over in another hour to talk in more details.

When Tank and Playa arrived at the house, Tyrone was hosting a party. There were about one hundred guests, and about eighty of them were young attractive females. The party was wild and rowdy, so Tyrone led the two to a quiet room. "This is better; at least I can hear myself," he said. "So are you the man for the operation?"

"Me and my partner talked it over and we like how it sounds," Tank said.

"Oh, so you work with a partner now?" Tyrone asked.

"Well, not really, cause actually he's my people. Anything I do, he does, and vice-versa."

Tyrone then said, "That's alright. Some people do it like that; ain't nothing wrong with that." He continued, "Congratulations, young blood, you've made a wise decision. You and your partner, oh, I mean your people, now own your own operation. As long as you're in the apartment complex, you won't have to worry about neither the police nor the goods. Now I'm going to get back to the party; after all, I am the host. Y'all stay and make yourselves at home. You can have anything or anyone you like and want, if you know what I mean."

At around 8:30 p.m., Solo, Pop, and Suga were at the gambling house hanging out, when they noticed the two young hustlers who were suppose to pay them protection money. Four more guys accompanied the two. Despite this, Pop walked over to them and demanded the money. Without any words said, the six guys attacked the Willowcreek members. It was an ugly sight; they got beat-up, disarmed and humiliated. They even were robbed for a little over a thousand dollars between the three of them.

Two minutes after the brawl, the three gathered enough composure to leave the gambling house. They tried to rush to the room before Mama saw them, but they were too slow. When she saw the boys' beat-up condition, her motherly instincts kicked in. She cleaned up all of their wounds. Surprisingly, she didn't even say a word while tending to them. However, after she patched them up, her questions and lecturing began.

"What happened to y'all? Look at your eyes, Malik! Dwayne and Kenneth, who y'all got into a fight with?" Suga said with one eye swollen shut, "We ain't fight nobody mama; we just got into a car accident."

Grandma knew that he was lying. "You think I'm a naive old lady? Stop lying to me, boy. What really happened?" Grandma realized that Suga wasn't going to tell her the truth. "You see what happened to y'all? That's a warning sign from God himself. I'm telling y'all that y'all need to stop hanging on those streets, because there's nothing but trouble out there. Y'all think that the money or them ol sleazy girls can save ya. Believe me, they'll be the furthest things from your mind. I'm not telling y'all this to be miserable, but because I want to share the good news to ya."

Suga couldn't stand to hear anymore. "Mama, thank you for cleaning us up, but would you be kind enough to let us rest?"

Grandma said, "I can't shove God down y'all's throat; the most I can do for y'all is to pray for you."

When Playa walked in the house, it was minutes after two in the morning. He jumped straight in his bed to knockout for the night. Just as he was getting comfortable, Suga entered his room. Playa hardly recognized him. "Damn cousin, what happened to you? It looks like your slave-owner caught you trying to escape the plantation."

Suga lowered his voice so Grandma couldn't hear. "Naw man, remember them cats y'all had jumped when Tank had came out of prison?"

Playa took a second to recollect on the incident. "Yeah, why?"

"Them nigga's jumped me, Solo, and Pop."

Playa couldn't hold in his laugh. "Boy, by the looks of you, them nigga's beat y'all down."

"It was six of them, and all of them were packing," Suga said in a defensive tone.

While still laughing, Playa said, "Boy lookit here, I hope Solo, and Pop don't look like you, because you look tore up, my nigga."

Suga slammed the door after that comment.

When Tank got home, it was also minutes after two. He thought to himself, I have the money, but I'm still missing something. He could not decipher what he was missing, but he knew that he felt lonely. Normally when Tank came home so late, he went straight to sleep, but for some strange reason, he felt the need to pray to God. It was a simple prayer and it sounded like this: "Lord, I'm not sure if you hear me, but if you do, please forgive me of my sins. Give me strength as I continue in this rat race. Grant me true happiness as I journey in this expedition. Please bless my friends and family I pray, amen." As soon as he concluded this, he felt as if a burden was removed from his shoulders. He was alone but strangely he didn't feel lonely anymore. Before he went to bed, he read Psalms 95.

At 8:00 a.m., Tank jumped out of bed because of a nightmare. He stayed in bed another five minutes just trying to interpret the meaning of the dream. He dreamed he was driving his car when a tornado appeared and swallowed his car. He was so scared that he woke up, not knowing if he lived or died in the dream. He wondered about the dream, but that was not a legitimate reason for him to postpone the day's affairs.

Tank and Playa met with Tyrone at noon. They each brought $2,500, to finalize the deal with Tyrone. After he gave them the merchandise, he escorted them to their building. As soon as they arrived, the two were making sales every three minutes. Tyrone spent around half an hour getting the two acquainted with the regular customers. Before Tyrone left the buildings, the new owners had made at least $1,500. Tank estimated that business would be busy enough for the other three members of the crew to reap the benefits also.

The two stayed there until 11:00 p.m. When they counted the money, they had made nearly $7,000 together. They knew that their products would be needed in the nights, so they arranged for the other three to work during the nights. The two were excited about their new investment, and the possibilities to make a large profit were endless. They went their separate ways, but agreed to meet up at the building the following morning.

The next morning, Tank was back at the building. He figured that he would go in early and consequently he would make a larger profit. Playa arrived at noon, and by that time, Tank had already made $ 2,500.

At 1:00 o'clock, Tank decided to go to McDonald's for lunch. While there, he saw Tameka eating lunch with her boyfriend. He felt vindictive, so he went over to them and started to flirt with Tameka. Her boyfriend almost lost his composure, but he knew that Tank wasn't a person whom he wanted to be an enemy with. When he and Tameka were leaving, Tank told her to stop by at his place sometimes. You could see the anger in the boyfriend's face as he realized that his girlfriend knew Tank on a personal level. Tank usually wasn't a troublemaker, but it was obvious that the money had boosted his ego.

Tank resumed his position and got back to work. This day was even faster than the day before, so he decided to leave early. He made $3,300 in a few hours time span. At the time, his philosophy was that money made a man, but he would soon change that philosophy.

Tank went straight to the gambling house. Although they had been attacked there, Solo, Pop and Suga were there. The four thugs talked about their new operation, but ceased all talking when they saw Pookie. He asked them all kinds of questions, as if he was trying to pry into their business. After he gave them the third degree, he told them that he had to go for a job interview.

Once out of their sight, he went to a payphone to call Santiago. When Pookie told Santiago that the guys were at the gambling house, he hung up the telephone and rushed there. Coincidentally, however, the guys had left a few minutes before Santiago and his lynch mob arrived. It can be called a vibe or good luck, but I prefer to call it divine intervention.

At 9:00 p.m., Tank brought his three friends to the building. Just as Tyrone did to him, he showed them around the complex, as well as introduce them to the drug users.

When Tank got home, the first thing he did was to call Tameka. Although he and Tameka weren't officially boyfriend and girlfriend, he was comfortable around her. Her answering machine picked up, and he was going to leave a message but he declined.

At 3:00 a.m., Tank was fast asleep when his telephone rang. He was going to let it ring out, but he decided to answer it just in case it was an urgent call. It was Solo and he told him that Red's funeral was going to be Saturday morning. After they hung up, Tank stayed awake for an hour, trying to figure out the meaning of life.

When Pookie heard about Red's funeral, he knew that the whole gang would be there. He didn't really want to ruin Red's funeral, but he didn't know if he would have another opportunity like this. He quickly called Santiago, and assured him that Tank would be at the funeral. Of course, Pookie wanted to know how and when he would receive his reward. Santiago told him that he would give him the money after he saw Tank with his own eyes.

At the exact time that Pookie was plotting, Tank and Playa were selling death to those that wanted a quick fix. Playa was usually rude to the feigns, but on that particular day he was quite polite with them. After a few hours at the building, they left and met up with the other guys. By this time, they all knew about the events of the following day. Ironically, they got into a discussion about life after death. Playa and Suga said that they believed in reincarnation. Solo and Pop believed that life is what you make of it while you are alive, and then you sleep, never to awake again. Tank admitted that this was an unanswered question for him that he often wrestled with.

Looking back in hind-sight, I can now understand why they chose this topic to discuss. This was the last time that the posse would all be together. They did not know it, but they were saying farewell to each other. They didn't make much money that day, but they did enjoy each other's company.

CHAPTER 5

FUNERAL TURNED MORGUE

Saturday, June 1st, was a peculiar day from the outset. The weather was rainy, and the mood was lousy. At 9:00 a.m., Tank woke up and began to get dressed for the funeral. By 9:45, all of the soldiers arrived at Tank's apartment. They waited for Pookie, but by 10:15, they decided to leave. Few words were spoken amongst the crew, but they managed to light up a joint on behalf of Red.

Once inside of the church, one couldn't help but to see Red's lifeless body lying motionless in a fancy casket. The pastor gave an electrifying sermon that gave Red's mother a bit of consolation. She tried to keep her composure, but she was obviously heartbroken as the pallbearers took away her only child.

If the mother seemed to be taking it bad at the church, at the cemetery is where she really lost it. The five street soldiers saw Pookie, looking as if he was in a daze. After the corpse was lowered into the ground and put into the dirt, everyone dispersed.

Santiago and four of his men were in a stolen car outside of the reception. They knew that their targets would soon arrive, so they each took a few swigs of some Hennessey. Santiago and his boys grew more anxious with every passing minute.

At last, cars started to fill the parking lot. When Solo's car came in, Santiago recognized his adversaries with Pookie. The Willowcreek members exited the car, and were walking towards the building. Santiago and his lynch mob approached their enemies with drawn guns. Without any words being exchanged, several shots were fired. Everyone was running and screaming, and bullets seemed to be flying everywhere. After about 20 seconds of terror, the bullets ceased. About twelve people lay on the ground, bleeding. The worst case scenario had happened on an already bad day.

When the paramedics arrived on the scene, four people were already dead. Three were critically injured, and five people had received non-life-threatening injuries. Among the dead were Playa and Pookie. Among the critically injured were Tank and Pop. Solo was struck in the leg, but it was not serious. The only member of the posse who managed to elude the bullets was Suga. In the short history of the posse, they had managed to commit several crimes, but now they were finally paying for them.

Ironically, Tank and Pop were airlifted to M.D. Sanderson. They both were unconscious and unaware of the tragedy which had taken place. Tank was struck twice, once in the neck and once in the leg. The doctors would have to run several different tests to accurately diagnose him, but they suspected that he was paralyzed from the incident. Although he was critically injured, they were able to stabilize him.

Pop was also struck twice. Both of the bullets entered through his stomach. His injuries were more severe, because one of his lungs collapsed, which made it difficult for him to breathe. He also lost a lot of blood due to the injury he sustained.

After the coast was clear, Suga rose up from the pavement. He knew that he had just survived a massacre. The first thing he did was to check if his comrades were all right. He first saw Solo, who was walking with a limp because of the bullet in his leg. Immediately after, they saw Tank and Playa, lying motionless next to each other. Pop was about a foot behind the two, but he too lay motionless. Pookie was even further away, and he also had sustained fatal injuries.

Suga and Solo were gangsters, but they had never experienced anything like this. The two were in a state of shock. Reality slapped Suga in the face as he heard that his cousin was dead. Suga knew that he had to tell the bad news to Grandma, before she heard about it from another source.

When Suga came home, Grandma knew that something was wrong because his shirt was covered with blood. With apprehension in her voice, she asked, "What's wrong? I know that something bad happened, what is it?"

Suga paused, hoping that he would awaken from a nightmare. "Mama, I don't know what happened. We were at a funeral and somebody just started to shoot it up."

She intervened and said, "What happened, where's Samuel at?"

Suga painstakingly answered while tears rolled down his face. "Mama, Playa got shot and died."

Grandma lost her composure and refused to be consoled.

Pop was rushed straight into the emergency room. The doctors worked frantically to stabilize his condition, but it only seemed to worsen. The only chance for his survival was by receiving a blood transfusion, but he had a rare blood type and while the hospital staff frantically tried to find it, he went into cardiac arrest, and shortly thereafter, took his last breath.

When Tank reached the hospital, the paramedics had already stabilized his condition. His body had suffered trauma, so they handled him with great care. They ran a series of tests on him, and confirmed what they had suspected; he had been paralyzed from a bullet which had struck his neck. It injured the fifth and sixth cervical bones. Therefore, they brought him to the intensive unit to monitor him overnight.

Back in Willowcreek, the news of the massacre spread like a wild forest fire. Somehow, the news made its way to Tameka. The person who relayed the message to her told her that Tank was one of the deceased. Although immediately before this incident, Tameka and Tank were not on speaking terms, she began to mourn for her gangster lover. She was so upset by the news that she cancelled her rendezvous with Derek. Since he didn't like Tank, he gave her an ultimatum; either she keep the date with him or forget about their relationship. She chose to break off the relationship and mourn over the late, and great, Tank.

Later that night, Tameka watched the local news report on the bloody massacre. She found out that Tank had survived the ordeal. Although she was relieved to find out that he had survived, she still couldn't help but feel worried for him. After the report, she called every local hospital, trying to find out his whereabouts. Because there had been an attempt to take his life, the hospital wouldn't disclose any information about him over the telephone. Before she went to bed, she said a prayer on behalf of Tank.

The next morning, Tank awoke from his state of unconsciousness. He was in a state of shock when he saw all of the IVs inserted into his body. He tried to rise out of bed, but he couldn't even budge. Now he was worried about his predicament. A few minutes later, a nurse came into the room to check on him. He asked her the reason he was in the hospital with severe pain. She was the first to let him know that he had been shot. It was funny, because the last thing he remembered was attending Red's funeral.

After the nurse gave him the overwhelming news about his condition, he asked her to call Playa for him. Suga answered the phone in a low-pitched voice. "Yeah?"

"What up man?" Tank said faintly. Suga recognized Tank's voice. "How you feeling, man?"

"Dog, I can't move! What happened man?" Suga laid it all out for him. "We were at Red's funeral and Santiago shot it up. Everybody got shot except for me."

"How's everybody else? Are they alright?"

Suga paused before answering. "Playa, Pop, and Pookie are all gone, man."

Tank felt sorry for himself, but after he heard the news about his friends, his self-pity was sidetracked. He waited about thirty seconds to gain his composure. "Hey, dog, I'm sorry. Tell Mama I'm very sorry and my condolences go out to y'all."

Immediately after Suga hung up the telephone, Tameka called him. She gave her condolences, but her real purpose for the call was to find out the whereabouts of Tank. Suga knew that she and Tank were close, so he gave her Tank's hospital telephone number.

She called Tank but no one answered the telephone. So she got dressed and went to the hospital to see him for herself. When she arrived, he was being prepped for surgery and already under anesthesia, so consequently he was incoherent. Although she couldn't enter the operating room, she made up her mind the stay the duration of the operation.

At 5:45 p.m., Tank woke up from his deep sleep. When Tameka noticed that his eyes were opened, she rose to her feet as if standing to a judge's entrance into a courtroom. Tank again noticed the IVs inserted into his body, so he asked her, "What happened? I thought you were mad at me."

Tameka just smiled at him and said, "I could never stay mad at you, Frank."

His face got stoic. "Tameka, I can't move. I think I got paralyzed, and Playa, Pop and Pookie got killed."

"Don't think so much, Baby. You need to rest up right now."

He looked at her with a stony face. "I don't need to rest. I'm alright but my homies ain't." Tears began to roll down his face. "If I didn't introduce them to Santiago, all of this wouldn't have happened. Why, God, did you let this happen?"

Tank was in depression over his paralysis and over the lost of his friends. Tameka tried to console him, but the news was too overwhelming for him to find any solace from her words. She stayed at the hospital a few hours before deciding to go home.

At about 7:00 p.m., Grandma came to the hospital to visit Tank. She was the last person that he expected to see, especially after she had lost her grandson so tragically. The first thing that she did was to give him a big kiss on the cheek. Tears rolled down her face as she said, "Thank God that you made it, son!"

Tank repeated, "Yeah, thank God, but I can't help but to feel guilty because I made it and my brothers didn't. Mama, I'm sorry about Playa. He was like my brother. I'm gonna miss him."

Grandma looked into the ceiling and whimpered, "I'm gonna miss my baby too, but everything is in God's hand." Tank could no longer hold in his anger and frustration. "No disrespect, Mama, but how can you say that everything is in God's hand when he just allowed three young men to disappear from us, like their lives were meaningless?" Grandma understood his anger, but she still had to correct him. "I know that you're upset, but believe me when I tell you that my heart aches over the death of those three boys! But God can't be mocked, because what a man sows, he will reap, meaning that if a man lives without God's grace, he is susceptible to the attacks of the devil."

Tank layed motionless on his back, just staring at the ceiling. All of this talk reminded him of the days of old, never to be seen again. "Mama, would you be offended if I tell you that I'm tired?"

"Not at all, Baby. You rest up and think about the reason that God has given you a second chance in life." She said a prayer for him before she went off into the night.

After Grandma left, Tank started to pray. He mostly prayed about his physical condition, but he also prayed for his friends and loved ones. His life had been spared, but now all he had to do was to find out why. He wondered if his mother had any knowledge about the unfortunate incident that had occurred. She was probably in a crack house somewhere, totally oblivious to her son's condition! He thanked God that he had placed two women in his life who were more precious than silver and gold. Tameka and Grandma meant more to him now than ever before.

He didn't sleep well that night; every few minutes he jumped out of sleep due to nightmares.

At 7:30 a..m.., Tank woke up for good out of his interrupted sleep. He tried to get out of bed, forgetting his paralysis, but when his body wouldn't budge, he was brought back to reality. Immediately he began to yell for the nurses to come to his assistance. During all of this commotion, his roommate woke up. "Hey, cuz, you're gonna have to learn some patience, because you're not gonna get nothing you want when you want it."

Tank responded, "For real. How long you been in here?"

"Man, it's been twelve weeks of hell for me. What about you?"

Tank answered, "Me and my homies got shot-up three days ago, and the next thing I know, I'm in here."

"Man it's about fifteen brothers that's laid up in here because of bullets! Do you believe that?"

Tank shook his head. "Damn man, I don't know what's wrong with us black folks. I just can't understand it!"

"Dog, I know what's wrong with us - we cursed! You can try to make sense of the whole situation if you want to, but the bottom line is that we are cursed," the roommate insisted.

Tank objected. "I don't really believe that, but I would agree that we got some serious problems."

The two young gangsters had got so wounded up in their conversation that they had forgotten to introduce themselves to each other.

"Hey dog, my name is Winston, but on the streets I'm known as Winnie Pooh."

Tank replied, "Oh yeah, I'm Frank but my homies call me Tank."

The two were deep into their conversation when the nurse finally came in to attend to Tank. When the two injured boys got out of bed, they went their separate ways.

Tank was a new patient, so the therapist assessed his physical limitations. He couldn't do anything but move his head; just trying to move his body was an exhausting task. The therapists were pleasant, but Tank felt depressed. He tried to convince himself that he was lucky to have escaped death, but on the other hand, he couldn't help but to count his loss. Within two weeks, he had lost four friends and his own body; it was quite understandable that he would be down.

By 3:00 p.m., Tank had finished his vigorous rehabilitation for the day. When they brought him back to the room, Tameka was there. She gave him a warm hug and asked him about his day. He told her, and to his surprise, it was like releasing some pressure off of his chest. She empathized with him, and gave him a supportive shoulder to lean on.

By 4:00 p.m., the nurses put him back into bed. Tameka sat at the edge of the bed and massaged his motionless legs. Looking into his eyes, she said, "I've been thinking about what you told me."

Tank wondered if his memory was also affected from the paralysis. "What did I tell you?"

"You said that I should choose between you and Derek." He

suddenly recalled their conversation. "Oh yeah."

"Well, I never doubted that I loved you, but I didn't think that I was in love with you. The other day Derek gave me an ultimatum. He said that if I came to see you, he would have nothing to do with me. I guess it's obvious that I chose your side. Lately I've realized that I love you, and want to be there for you, as your friend, lover," she paused before concluding the sentence, "and your girlfriend."

Tank was speechless, so she continued. "I realized how much I loved you when we didn't speak to each other for those days. Even though Derek was there, I was miserable without you. I tried to forget about you, but the more I tried, the more I thought about you. When I came to your house and saw those girls there, I felt as if you were cheating on me. I know that I want to be with you, Frank."

Tank was honored by what he had just heard. "If I could hug you, I would," he said.

So she leaned over his bed and gave him his wish. He continued, "I'm glad you said that, Baby, because I feel the same way towards you, but I'm saying, I can't even stand up!"

Tameka put her hands over his mouth before he could say anything else. "Just you being with me is enough, but I know that you'll stand and walk again. In a strange way, I think that this is God's way of getting us together."

Without thinking, he reached to hold her close to him, and for the first time in three days, his left arm moved. He reacted as if he had seen a ghost. "You saw that, Baby? My hand moved a little bit!"

She shared his enthusiasm. "Yeah, Baby, I saw that! I told you that you're gonna beat this!"

Coincidentally, Grandma came into the room with her bible in her hand. When she saw that Tank and Tameka were hugging and kissing, she let her presence be known. "Is it alright if I come in, or should I come back?"

Tank said, "Come in, Mama!"

Tameka cut Tank off. "Frank just moved his hands Maam!" Now the excitement spread to Grandma. "Oh Baby, I'm so happy for you! Praise God!"

Tank watched his hands as they moved at will. "Yes, I do praise God for this!"

Grandma smiled. "This is just the beginning, because I know that God is going to put you back on your feet and change your life around."

Tank, being full of faith, said, "I believe you, Mama. I know that God is gonna work a miracle in my life."

Grandma and Tameka stayed a few more hours, celebrating with Tank, but by 8:00 p.m., he was noticeably weary. So first Grandma left, then shortly thereafter, Tameka went on her way.

CHAPTER 6

LIFE-ALTERING DREAM

Tank decided to retire for the night, and wake up early the following morning to vigorously work out. About two hours into his sleep, he had a dream that would stick with him for life.

The setting was unclear. It was a place that was unfamiliar to him. The person whom he conversed with spoke with a great deal of authority. Tank could tell that he possessed a great deal of power. Tank didn't get to see his face, because during the whole conversation, his face was towards the ground. The reason that he was in this position was because he revered the man that spoke to him, and also because of the light which shone from this gentleman's face.

The conversation went as follows: "Frank, why do you resist me?"

Tank answered with a question of his own, "Who are you sir?"

"I AM. The God of Abraham, Isaac, and Jacob."

Tank stuttered, "L-lord, how do I resist you?"

"I knew you before you were conceived in your mother's

womb. Many times I've tried to get your attention, but you wouldn't respond to my calling. So in order to get your attention, I have allowed these things which you have put on yourself to transpire. Even though your mother and father may forsake you, I am at your side. Think of everything good that has happened in your life." Instantaneously, everything that was good in Tank's life flashed before his face.

"I caused these things to happen. I was also carrying you when you were hopelessly in despair. Remember throughout this whole ordeal, that I am at your side. And though trials and tribulations will try to make you lose faith, don't give in. See, I have replaced your birth mother by giving you two women in your life. You must now receive instructions from my servant whom you call Grandma. Go now and repent of your sins and release the noose from your neck that so easily entangles. Then, share your faith with Tameka and also to the gangsters. I have chosen her to be one with you. I have chosen you to be a witness to a wicked and murderous generation. Go now and do as I say. Look back no more. Only keep your eyes on me and I will guide you."

When Tank woke up the following morning, the dream still lingered in his head. Ever since the shooting, he had been having nightmares, but this dream seemed to be real. It was sort of like he had entered another dimension.

Two months after the shooting, Tank's physical condition had improved tremendously. He now had the use of both of his hands. He also was standing upright with the assistance of a walker. Although he couldn't take any steps, if his progress continued at that speed, he was expected to eventually walk with little or no assistance.

His spirituality had also blossomed in this time period. He obediently did as the man in his dreams instructed him to do. He received teachings from Grandma, and within a month, he began to share his new faith to Tameka first, and then to everyone he came in contact with.

Nine weeks after the infamous day, Suga finally visited Tank in the hospital. Tank was standing, while Tameka was sitting on his bed, reading a scripture. Suga said, "Yo, what's up, Tank?"

Tank was surprised to see him. "You're what's up! I thought you and Solo forgot about me."

"Naw man, you're suppose to know that the last little bit has been hectic for all of us." Suga was trying to justify the reason he hadn't visited Tank sooner.

Tank said, "Yeah, I know cuz. It has been a little hectic lately, but how are you doing now?"

"Well I'm doing better now, but it still ain't the same without you, Playa, and Pop. I just wish that we could take back that day, and go back to normal."

Tank felt his pain. "Yeah man, that day still plays out in my mind from time to time."

Suga quickly changed the subject. "Word is on the street that that nigga, Pookie, set us up!"

Hearing this was like pouring salt into a wound that was just trying to heal. "Do you believe that, dog?"

Suga's facial expression turned into rage. "Yeah, I remember right before the shooting, he use to always want to know what we did and where we were going to be. Yeah, that punk nigga set us up. I hope he rots in hell!"

Tank didn't want to believe it, although it made sense. "I don't know, man. So what, are you still out there slanging and banging?"

Suga looked at Tameka before he answered. "You know, ain't nothing changed for me. I'm Willowcreek till I die, just like Playa and Pop."

Tank said, "Don't take this personal, but it ain't no future in that, my nigga."

Tameka added, "Yeah, Suga, every outlaw ends up with a tragic story."

Suga rationalized his decision by saying, "Man, too many of my peoples dun died on the streets like martyrs for me to back out now, and besides, I have a bone to pick with a few people."

Tank signaled for Tameka to help him sit back down on the bed. "No lie, dog, we were disillusioned before. We were fighting for no real cause. God spared our lives for a reason, so we just got to count our losses and move on."

"What you mean move on? Man, that was my cousin that they killed. I can't move on until I avenge his death, and then I can think about that, but until then, nigga, I'm wilding!"

"What good is it gonna do if you kill whoever? Tameka said. "You ain't gonna bring back Playa. Look, I lost my cousin to gang violence a few years ago, so I know what you're feeling inside, but it ain't gonna help if you kill. It will just be a continuous cycle, and within a few days or weeks, they'll be looking to kill you."

Suga looked at Tameka, then Tank. "You my man, dog, but for real, you dun switched up on a nigga. I just came by to see how you're doing, but I got to be running now."

It was Tank's last day at the hospital. Physically, he was making a little improvement daily. He could now walk with the assistance of two crutches. He hadn't improved one hundred percent, but he was still grateful.

Spiritually, he was ready to share his faith to the gangsters as he had been instructed to do in the dream. Although Tank was suppose to be teaching Tameka, they both seemed to excelling in their spirituality.

Exactly three months after the shooting, Tank left the hospital and headed home. With the help of the hospital, he moved from Willowcreek into a quieter apartment complex, about fifteen miles away.

When he reached the apartment, he grabbed Tameka's hand and said, "I thank you for being by my side the last three months. By far, that was the hardest situation I have ever faced in my life. If you weren't there, I don't know how I would have managed. You've proven to me that you're the best thing that has happened to me in this life, and I don't want you to ever leave me. I been thinking about this for a while, but I was waiting for the right moment to mention it. W-would you? What I'm trying to say is, would you do me the honor of being my wife?"

Tameka almost knocked him over with excitement. "You don't even have to wait for an answer! Sure I'll marry you Frank!"

They hadn't had sex in over three months, but contrary to their beliefs, their relationship grew more intense. Actually, the pre-mature sex seemed to have complicated the relationship between them in the past. They both agreed that they would wait until after they were married to have sex with each other. In that way, they would be obeying God's command, and it would also be more exciting if they waited until they were man and wife to unite in a sexual way.

Tameka spent the night on Tank's sofa bed. When they woke up, she made a continental breakfast for her fiancé and herself. After breakfast, Tank gave Grandma a call to see how she was doing. Suga answered. "Who this is?" "How are you doing brother? It's Frank." Frank was glad to hear Suga's voice.

Suga said, "I'm alright man. I heard that you left the hospital. Congratulations man. I don't know if you spoke to Solo yet, but we're having a little party on behalf of Playa and Pop on Saturday. Won't you come? I'm sure that the homies would love to see you there."

Before they hung up, Frank agreed to come by.

He told Tameka about the party, so she agreed to go with him. He knew that it would be tempting for him to return to his old setting, but he kept the life-changing dream in his mind. Tameka was going to work, so Frank asked her to drop him off at Willowcreek, so he could witness to the drug dealers.

The first place that Frank went to was the drug dealers' paradise. A couple of the dealers recognized him. "Yo! What's up homie? How's it been?"

Frank answered, "I can't complain. God has been good to me."

The older dealer asked Frank, "Is you back serving my nigga?"

Frank looked embarrassed. "Naw, man, I don't do that no mo. Actually, what I came for is to speak some knowledge to y'all."

The younger dealer showed Frank some respect. "Say big dog, you want a blunt while you speak?"

Frank knew that the gesture was respectful. "Naw little man, the reefer be having us disillusioned. We weren't born getting high, so why do it now when we're closer to death? What I want to talk about is the love that God has for us."

Just then, the older thug ran over to a drug addict and made a quick interaction with him. He ran back to his two visitors and said, "My fault, dog, you came at a busy time." Frank said, "Well I'll be quick. You see the sun, moon, stars, trees, animals, and all the people? God made it all. You can't even start to imagine how awesome he is. He made everyone of us to worship him. That's the duty of men and women. He predestined all of us to go to heaven, but sin entered the world and destroyed that."

The older thug said, "It was probably suppose to be like that, but it sure ain't like that no mo. So I got to go with the flow and get mines."

The younger thug interjected, "Then how do you explain all the good nigga's that be getting smoked? Did God intend it to be like that?"

Frank said, "I don't claim to have all the answers, but I know that we bring on a lot of the tragedies that happen to us. God gave everyone his or her own will, and some of us use it as a license to kill. It's not fair to blame the mistakes of others on God."

The older thug cut the conversation short. "Hey dog, I'd love to sit and chat, but time is money. Are you going to be at Solo's house on Saturday?"

"Yes."

"Well I'll see you there, and then we can finish our conversation."

Frank walked to the convenience store to get a bottle of juice. On his way out of the store, he ran into Solo and Roketta. "Yo what's up, Tank? You finally made it back to the hood."

"Yeah man, things ain't changed much over here."

Solo smirked, "Naw man, ain't nothing gonna change but the faces. Did you hear about the get-together at my house on Saturday?"

Frank shook his head yes.

"Well come over and I'll personally take care of everything for you, but right now I gotta shoot on the other side of town right quick."

Frank spent another hour in his old neighborhood, but everyone was too busy to listen. After three months of his absence from Willowcreek, he thought he would receive more attention than that. He also realized that he had a harder task in front of him than he originally thought it would be. It seemed as if everyone was content with their life of sin. He went home discouraged at the day's results.

The first thing he did as he got home was pray for the strength to carry on. After an hour in prayer, he fell into a deep sleep.

Once sleeping, Frank started to dream. The dream was of an old wise man. I'm assuming that he was wise, because the setting was in a classroom, and the man was the teacher. One by one, he gave each student different instructions to perform. When he made his way to Frank, he said, "I've given each student a different assignment. They're all different, but equally important. Your assignment is to speak to the thugs of your generation. It breaks my heart to see them behaving in such a manner. It's going to be hard, but when you get discouraged, remember that everyone who lives Godly will suffer persecution. But don't lose heart because the devil's plans will not prosper."

The man said, "Follow me." Immediately he was out of the classroom and on an island filled with beautiful fruits. "I've given you a helpmate to help ease the burden you will bear on earth. Just like you, I've chosen Tameka from birth to spread my good news to this murderous and adulterous generation. For a time she went astray, indulging in the pleasures of sin, but nevertheless, my word will not return to me void. I have removed the veils from her eyes so she will love you as you are. It is wise of you to marry her, for I've destined that from the foundations of the world. So faint not, for great is your reward in Heaven."

The man said once more, "Follow me." Immediately he was off the island and into a barren wilderness. Snakes were everywhere. What made it even more strange was the fact that the snakes sang as beautiful as angels. The man continued, "I know that you are amongst poisonous snakes with the voices of archangels, but beware, for none of them can be trusted. What I've called you to do is dangerous, but for my name's sake, you must witness to this wicked group, so that they have no excuses at my judgement. Although they seem intimidating, you must walk straight and narrowly through them to get to the other side."

All of a sudden just beyond the snakes, the island filled with beautiful fruits reappeared. Frank then walked through the snakes in order to get to the island. While he was walking, the snakes were laughing and cursing at him. As he was passing through the last snake, it hurled towards his heel and bit it. Although it bruised his heel, Frank crushed the snake's head before he made it to the island.

Right then there was a knock at the door. When Frank answered, Tameka came in. Frank was elated to see her, especially after the disturbing vision.

Tameka laughed as he hugged her tightly. "I know that you love me, but I didn't know this much."

Frank assured her that he did, and gave her a rundown on his dream.

It was ironic, because while she was driving home the night before, Tameka had been thinking that it would take a dream for her and Frank to marry each other. They had discussed it between themselves and also with Grandma, and had come to the conclusion that they would tie the knot in a month's time.

On Saturday morning, Frank woke up early, just as the sun penetrated the blinds and illuminated the entire room. As was his custom, he started the day off by saying a prayer.

By 10:00a.m., Tameka came to Frank's house with a hot plate of food. Frank was in the midst of getting dressed when he answered the door. They started to caress each other in a sexual manner, and kiss each other as if the next step was to head for the bedroom. Rather than succumb to temptation, Frank stopped and said, "We can't."

Tameka looked at him with a guilty look on her face, "You're right. I don't know what got into me."

"There's no need to be sorry; the same thing that got into you was in me. Before we eat breakfast, let's pray that God purges the spirit of lust that just came over us."

Tameka agreed, "Yeah because it almost successfully tempted us."

For the rest of the time before the party started, they courted each other in an innocent and godly manner. One of the things that they did was to further prepare for their wedding. They also asked each other to define family, and whether they would have kids, and if yes, how many. Next, they listed the reasons that they were in love with each other. The last thing they did before going to the party was pray that God's glory would be manifested.

When they arrived at Solo's house, quite a few people were already there. They wasted no time witnessing to the partygoers. A few people tried to act polite by listening, but the majority of people didn't want to talk about God. For the most part, everyone thought that the two disciples were crazy, and so they were outcast by the partygoers. Even some of Frank's old friends avoided him because they didn't want to talk righteous. After the two noticed that they weren't wanted, they politely said goodnight and departed.

On the way home, Frank was reading the bible and coincidentally came across Mark 6:4 which says, "A Prophet is not without honor, but in his own country and among his own kin and in his own house." That was a confirmation that he had to witness in other areas and not only in Willowcreek. He knew that he had made enemies in other areas, but he knew within himself that he had to do this.

The following morning, Grandma called Frank at 8:30a.m.. This was the first time since Frank could remember, that he was going to church. Grandma wanted to arrive no later than a quarter after ten. She had just called Frank to be his alarm clock. Initially, Frank was apprehensive about attending church. He sort of felt as if he would be out of place, but Grandma convinced him that a true Christian enjoys going to the house of GOD. So obediently he agreed with his mentor, but of course he convinced Tameka to come along.

Immediately after the phone call from Grandma, Frank

called Tameka. She had similar fears about attending church. Unlike Tank though, she had visited a couple of churches over the years but she had felt uncomfortable. Although she feared it somewhat, she was willing to go. She told Frank that she would get ready and be over in an hour.

When they arrived at the church, Frank and Tameka were impressed by its size. It had the capacity to hold around 500 people. By the looks of it, there were maybe 350 people there. Grandma led the way to the front, greeting everyone she passed. The two young people followed behind her like little children in a large mall.

Once they took their seats, Sunday school began. The teacher of the class taught with energy and enthusiasm. One could tell that he was an articulate and effective talker. He talked about the last days with great clarity. Even though he used big words, he made sure he explained his statements. The Sunday school class lasted about 50 minutes and was followed by a short intermission before the actual service.

During the intermission, Grandma introduced her two guests to several members. She made the two feel comfortable and the church members seemed to welcome them with open arms. She also told the members that the two were fiancées, only three weeks from marriage.

The Pastor was less articulate than the Sunday school teacher, but he possessed a certain charisma that made his sermon electrifying. He preached about Abraham's obedience to GOD. He said, "Although Abraham didn't have a bible to read about faith, he was credited for believing GOD. And as a result, he became the father to many nations, kindreds and races of people." During the sermon, people were shouting, raising their hands and speaking in tongues. It seemed as if everyone in the building was getting emotional. Even a few times Frank unconsciously raised his hands in reverence to GOD. What made it even more electrifying was the fact that the organs were being played during the sermon.

Frank and Tameka were glad they had come. After the service, a member of the congregation introduced himself to Frank and Tameka. He had noticed Frank's physical condition, It just so happened that he was a business owner who hired disabled employees. He and Frank exchanged numbers and he agreed to give Frank an interview. He told Frank that when he called the office, he was to ask to speak with Mr. Jones. The next morning Frank called Mr. Jones to set up an interview. Mr. Jones told Frank that the next morning would be perfect. When Frank got off of the phone, he praised and glorified GOD for this opportunity. He hadn't been given a position yet, in fact he hadn't even had an interview, but he felt an assurance that he would get the job.

At about 11:00 a.m., Tameka came over to Frank's apartment. As always, before she entered the house, she gave him a welcoming kiss. This was Tameka's day off so she had predetermined the couple's day. First they would go to the park to spend some time with each other and the Lord. Then they would go to the mall and look for wedding rings. Finally, they would rent a movie and go back home to watch it. They both enjoyed spending time with each other.

Once at the park, they both went to a secluded area and with no delays, they began to make their petitions known to the Lord. They spent an hour making petitions, interceding and asking for guidance. When they were finished praying, they went for a long walk. While they were walking, they were talking to each other. They took a 30-minute walk and afterward rested for 30 minutes.

Tameka knew that Frank had foes at the Bluepoints area, so she chose to pass that mall and go to another one. When they arrived, they looked in every jewelry shop. Frank noticed a specific ring had caught Tameka's attention. She was a very humble lady, so she didn't tell Frank that she wanted it but he noticed the twinkle in her eye when she saw it. He made it a point to get a card from the store and also to remember the price. As they left the mall, they were surprised to find that they had been there for over 3 ½ hours.

It was obvious that they were very much in love with each other and that this was a simple but romantic day for the couple. So instead of renting an action movie, they mutually agreed to rent a romantic movie. Before they went back to Frank's apartment to watch it, they stopped at McDonald's to get a bite to eat.

They had planned on being celibate until the day of their marriage, but they got carried away with lust. The way it started was because they were cuddled up and before they knew it, they were touching each other. Then they were kissing, touching and cuddling. Then the clothes were off and to be honest, neither of them tried to fight the feeling.

Immediately after, they both felt guilty. It was as if they were Adam and Eve and had just taken a bite of the forbidden fruit. They understood that the spirit was willing but the flesh was weak and they made a vow they would not fall by the way of that temptation again.

Later on that night, Suga and Solo made an unexpected visit. When they came in, Frank couldn't help but notice the extravagant clothes that they were wearing. They wore more gold than Mr. T. in his prime.

Suga said, "How you doing, dog? I'm just gonna be forward. You down forever and well, you can probably tell business is good. We wanted to know if you wanted to come back and make some money?"

Frank shook his head as he said, "Man y'all know I ain't down with that no mo."

Suga continued, "I know you could use some extra cash; Momma told me that you're engaged."

Frank stood his ground. "GOD will provide for me. I don't need no blood money."

Solo got offended. "Niggas been saying that you done went crazy, but now I know it's true! Man, you better quit tripping and get with the program, nigga."

Frank responded in an argumentative tone of voice, "For your information, y'all the one's that's trippin. Y'all selling death to the brothers and sisters and making a profit off of it." Solo said in a frustrated tone, "Man, I ain't got time to hear this junk. I'm out."

Suga held the door open as he said, "I understand if you got your beliefs. I didn't mean to offend you. You know we been down from day two, so I had to at least offer you a piece of the pie. But if you ever change your mind, you know you're down."

When Suga left, you could see the frustration in Frank's eyes. Even though he held his position firmly, he honestly could use some fast cash. The ring that Tameka liked was $3,000.00 and he was used to having the finer things in life. But he had made up his mind that he wasn't going to participate in any illegal activities to earn money. He would rather live humbly and do without certain things than to sell his soul for vanity.

The following morning, Frank was awakened by the phone. He was elated to hear Tameka wishing him good luck on his interview. She also tried to alleviate some of the anxiety he had concerning the interview. You see, Frank had never been on an interview so he was apprehensive about it. Tameka gave him a little mock interview to assure him that it wouldn't be as hard as he was making it out to be. They talked for a few more minutes before Frank got ready for his first, and hopefully only, job interview.

At 10:30a.m. Tameka arrived at Frank's door to bring him to the interview. On the way there, she tried to relax his mind by conversing with him but Frank seemed to be meditating about the interview. Tameka would say something or ask a question but he would only respond with as few words as possible. So after a few attempts, she also kept silent, understanding the change in his attitude.

When Frank met Mr. Jones for the interview, Mr. Jones could tell that he was nervous. He assured Frank that there was nothing to worry about. He also complimented Frank on his wardrobe, boosting up his confidence. He started off by giving Frank an application to fill out. When Frank had completed it, Mr. Jones asked him a few questions. "How long have you been injured?"

"About five months now."

"How do you feel about your disability?"

"Well, the way I see it is this is a blessing in disguise. I lost three friends during the incident and I could easily be dead and buried right now, too"

"Do you feel that you can be an encouragement to people with disabilities, like senior citizens and people that are suicidal?"

Frank answered, "Well, honestly I believe I could for the simple reason that while there is life, there is hope. And I can relate to all of them because I am disabled. My body functions are like that of a senior citizen, and believe it or not, before I had this hope, I was suicidal."

Mr. Jones was impressed with the answers he had heard. He hadn't realized it before but Frank was a very intelligent young black man. He was up out of his seat, congratulating Frank for successfully concluding his interview. Frank was proud of himself, and thanked GOD because he knew that he had kept his composure. Mr. Jones confirmed his success by asking, "Can you start working tomorrow from 9 to 5?"

"I would like that sir," Frank said.

"Great! I can use a positive young man such as yourself."

At that exact time, Tyrone was conspiring with some officers to shut down Willowcreek's drug operation. The remnant of the posse seemed to be getting too large and he was afraid they would eventually turn on him. He gave the officers vital information about the operation that only he knew. The drug business is a dirty game and not even your allies can be trusted.

When the officers came to the building where Tyrone had confirmed the posse would be, three paddy wagons arrived with several swat team officers. When they entered the building, they made everyone lie face down on the ground. They arrested 38 people, mostly drug addicts. When they identified the people, they realized that they hadn't apprehended the main suspects they came for. They promised to release one of the addicts if he would tell them were Suga and Solo resided. Like I said, it's a dirty game, so within an hour, the officers were kicking down Suga and Solo's door. They still didn't find them but they seized a large amount of drugs and weapons. Then warrants were drawn up for the two thugs.

Solo was the first of the two to find out about the sweep. A neighborhood wino had witnessed the raid and because Solo was always giving him money, he informed him about the raid. Solo then told Suga about the bad news. Suga blew a fuse when he heard. He said that he knew that Tyrone had something to do with it and vowed to pay him back. The only problem was that he didn't know where Tyrone lived, but he knew that Tank knew.

When Tyrone learned about the bust, the first thing out of his mouth was, "Did you get them?" The police officer said, "We arrested 38 people," avoiding the specific question. Tyrone repeated, "Did you get them?" The officer finally confessed, "No they were not there."

Tyrone yelled, "What do you mean you didn't get them!" The officer said, "I don't know, but they weren't there." Tyrone said in an aggravated voice, "I pay you guys so much and y'all can't even arrest two little punks!" The officer retaliated, "Look, we're officers not GOD. We even went to their house but neither of them was there." Tyrone regained his senses. "I'm sorry, it's just that these kids are wannabe cowboys and they'll come after me." The officer responded, "Don't worry, we got warrants out for them. They'll be in our custody in a matter of time." Tyrone ended the conversation by saying, "I hope so."

Meanwhile, Frank was still basking in his victorious interview and was in the middle of praying when he heard a loud banging at the door. When he answered it, Suga entered looking real scary. "Yo I'm glad you're here! I got a problem and I need you to help me."

Frank said, "Why, what's up?"

Suga gave Frank a run down on the drug bust and said that Tyrone was the informant.

Frank asked, "Then what do you want me to do?"

"I need to know Tyrone's address."

"Look here, dog, I really can't get involved!" Frank said.

Suga's eyes widened as he said, "This ain't no joke man..... that nigga crossed me and you're gonna tell me where he live, either voluntarily or with force!" He put a pistol into Frank's side as he said it.

Frank was stubborn but not stupid and even though he didn't want to get involved, he could tell that Suga was dead serious. So he reluctantly told Suga Tyrone's address. After Frank told him, Suga said, "I didn't mean to scare you but I had to get his address."

Frank didn't speak aloud but he knew that a war was going to break out and that Suga was headed for a downfall.

Before Suga left, he said "Hey man, I'll pay you cash when all of this is settled."

Frank didn't look in Suga's eyes as he said, "That's alright Malik, but be careful and remember that it's never too late to turn to GOD." By the time he had said that, Suga was gone out the door.

Suga called Solo on his celullar phone and arranged to meet up privately. When they met, Suga said to Solo "Tonight's the night that Tyrone goes out of business... permanently." Solo didn't even bother to ask Suga what he meant because he already knew. He knew that amongst the whole crew, he had more say than Suga, but right now, Suga led and Solo followed.

They layed low until sundown and then they hit the scene. They first stopped off at Smiley's to get two guns and a bulletproof vest for each of them. Then they got a large bag of reefer.

At 10:00 p.m., Suga decided that it was time to retaliate. They rented one of the crack addicts' cars for the night since the cops had seized each of theirs. There was no talking between the two; they just smoked and absorbed the music. Before they arrived at the house, they shook each other's hand, ghetto style.

Solo followed behind as Suga made his way to the door. Suga looked back and said to Solo, "Follow me." In one kick, the door slammed open. Before shooting, they saw Tyrone and three more men. One man reached for his gun and then the gunshots began. Bullets were flying back at them, so the two thugs had to retreat. The two let off a few more shots before they sped away in the waiting car.

After all of the thug life, they were worse off than when they had started. Besides being broke, they had lost close friends and family members and now they were wanted dead or alive. They both agreed that they had to leave town and separate. They hugged and wished each other luck before they went their separate ways.

When Frank woke up the next morning, he prayed.

Afterward he turned on the news as he usually did before work. He was dumbfounded when he saw Solo and Suga's faces on the news. The reporter said, "The two suspects entered into the house and emptied their guns at the four shocked men. Luckily, one of the men was a police officer who drew his revolver and fired back at the assailants. This move saved their lives. The two rogues cowered out and left running, not even able to carry out their robbery scheme." Then the reporter gave their description and warned the public that these guys were known gang members and very ruthless.

Immediately, Frank bowed down on his knees and prayed for his two ex-homies. He was aware of the anger and fear that they must have been feeling. He was deeply saddened by the outcome of the whole situation.

After he finished his prayers, he reflected on the outcome of Willowcreek posse. He remembered the day that he came out of prison and met with the rest of the gang. The posse seemed to be prospering but that was only temporary. He thought about Playa. He reminisced about the early years, right up to the more recent days. He thought about Pop. Pop always made everyone hype. He remembered Suga, Solo, Pookie and even thought about himself. He reasoned with himself that the posse must have made a deal with the devil, because three of them were dead, one disabled, and now the remaining two were on the run.

He felt bad, but he still had to go to work. By the time Tameka arrived to drive him to work, Frank was ready to go. He didn't bother to tell Tameka the news about Suga and Solo. He wanted to clear his mind of any negative news in order to focus on his job.

At work, Frank kept his composure and the day went by nicely. After work, he decided to witness at the Bluepoints apartments, his ex-arch-rival gang's headquarters. Frank was there for about five minutes when he saw two guys whom he recognized. They were two members of Bluepoints posse. When they saw him, they noticeably got tense. Frank said, "Don't worry, brothers. I've come here in peace." The two thugs hadn't seen him since he got paralyzed, but they heard that he was messed up. One of the thugs laughed as he said, "Where all your boys at man?"

Frank knew that he already knew the answer, so he said, "I don't know. Why, do you know?"

The thug took a pull of his joint as his face got serious and he replied, "Yeah, half of them niggas is dead and the other half is on the run, so I guess you're the only punk nigga still left standing," He started to laugh again when he finished, "and you ain't even doing that right!"

Frank now knew with certainty that his presence wasn't welcomed. "Look, I'm just here to spread some light with you."

The other thug finally joined in, "I don't think we want the same light as y'all." This time both of them began to laugh.

Frank continued, "The light that I'm talking about is Jesus Christ, the one and only true light."

The thug interrupted again. "I don't think you understand. You're from Willowcreek and this is Bluepoints' turf." He continued, "I tell you what I'll do, I'll let you hop out of here without getting a well deserved butt whipping."

Tank was aware of the threat. "I no longer represent Willocreek. I am now an ambassador for Christ. So you can do whatever, but know that you're fooling with GOD's property." The two guys were shocked at the courageous response. Frank continued, "I know that at one time we were arch rivals but now I approach y'all as brothers in Christ. Just like y'all, I was once deceived and misled, but GOD has shed his light on me and I no longer walk in darkness."

One of the thugs asked him, "So are you trying to say that I'm walking in darkness?"

Frank thought before he spoke. "I'm simply saying that anyone who doesn't walk according to GOD's law is in darkness."

The thug responded, smiling, "Well then, maybe I am walking in darkness." He continued, "I would love to stay and chat but I'm on official business. But I'm gonna tell you that you should be careful around here, because I don't know if the other niggas will be as calm as us." They walked away after giving Frank the warning.

Frank stayed at the Bluepoint apartments witnessing for around four hours. He saw faces that he remembered, but no one had time in their busy schedule to hear about Christ. Most people who saw Frank getting around with his crutches felt sorry for him, but ironically, Frank felt sorry for them.

When Tameka came to pick Frank up, he was relieved to see a receptive and friendly face.

"How was your day, Baby?" she asked him while he was buckling his seat belt.

"I've had better ones." Frank answered.

"What's wrong Frank? You don't sound that good," she said in a concerned voice. Frank filled Tameka in on the news about Suga and Solo. Tameka felt bad to hear the news, but she wasn't surprised.

Around 10:00 p.m., Solo received a call on his cellular phone from a girl he knew. He was sort of surprised to hear from her, but she was too good looking for him not to talk to her. They spoke about everything at first, and then she told him that she would like to see him. Not thinking cautiously, Solo accepted the invitation. They agreed that her place was a good spot to carry out their rendezvous. At around 11:00 p.m., Solo was ready to carry out his date with destiny. He knew that he should be as cautious as possible, but he had convinced himself that he needed female companionship.

Solo didn't even notice the parked van with the tinted windows across the street from the girl's house. But when he knocked on the door, he heard the van door slide open. By the time he turned around, seven swat team officers were running at him with drawn weapons. He still tried to run, but like in most movies, he fell. By the time he got up, the police had swarmed him like ants on a lonely dead bug. I guess Solo was unlucky and lucky. Unlucky, because from that time on he was in captivity, and lucky because they didn't shoot him. When the girl who lived there came outside, she quickly looked at Solo and said to the officers, "That's him." Solo became angry at this and couldn't restrain his mouth. "You better watch your back, girl! You done messed up!"

Around the same time, Suga was halfway across Louisiana. He had family in Orlando, Florida, so that was his destination. He was experiencing a feeling of apprehension, but he had no other choice but to go to a place that he knew nothing about. He still had a long bus ride, so he slept off a little of his anxiety.

Later on that same night, Tameka decided to keep Frank company, seeing that he was upset about the news of his friends. When she arrived, he was reading some scriptures in Psalms, seeking guidance. So she joined into the bible study. Afterward they just cuddled up to watch TV for the remainder of the night. Their wedding was scheduled for exactly two weeks from that day, so they also made out a few more invitation cards to potential guests.

When Tameka fell asleep, Frank stayed awake and began to ponder on the meaning of life. He wondered if he would ever receive his full strength back. He thought about how blessed he was to have a beautiful, intelligent, ambitious and God-fearing fiancée like Tameka. He thought about GOD and the unlimited power that He possesses. He meditated for nearly two hours on his bed about these matters.

The next morning, Frank woke up bright and early and he read a few scriptures. When Tameka woke up, she did the same, and also prepared breakfast for the two. It was Sunday morning, so they did everything with speed in order to attend Sunday school. Before they left, Frank called Grandma to see if she wanted them to pick her up and bring her to church. When she answered, she told him she didn't sleep much the night before, and as a result, she wouldn't be going to church. She told Frank to pray for her in her absence and Frank agreed. He told her that he and Tameka would visit her after the service.

Solo didn't sleep much that night either, and as you can imagine, he was up early as well. When all the prisoners were let out of their cells, Solo went to the phone to call Roketta. As he was dialing the number, another prisoner told him he needed to use the phone.

Solo said, "I won't be that long." The guy pressed the button and said," What I mean is that I need the phone right now!" Solo had never been to jail, so he didn't understand that a phone call could cause such a big deal. He continued, "Look man, I'm just gonna call my woman right quick, and let her know that I'm alright." The prisoner still wasn't satisfied with the answer, and reached for the phone. In one motion, Solo smacked the phone in the guy's face, and they started fighting. The guy was the biggest convict in that section, and no one had ever challenged his authority. Yet Solo was too mad to care about his size. It wasn't long until the guards separated the two, and being that the other guy had been there for one month without any incident, to the guards it seemed as if Solo had provoked the fight. Although Solo tried to plea his case, they didn't believe him, and so Solo's first few hours in jail brought him a fight which landed him in solitary confinement for five days.

By this time, Suga was a few hours from his destination. He had had a lot of time to think about what he had done, and the possible consequences. He was so deep in thought that he neglected eating for the whole bus trip. All he could think about is the pain this gang life had brought to his grandmother; and the bad thing about it was that she didn't condone it in the least. At this point, GOD seemed to be the only one who would understand the mental anguish that he was going through.

At the church, the Pastor preached about the "Last Days". He referred mainly to "Revelations" but he did touch on Matthew and Luke. This information particularly interested Frank, because by the way the preacher was illustrating the prophesies, it seemed evident that these were the last days. This sermon left Frank with an urgency to preach the gospel to the gang members who were totally ignorant to this revelation. Tameka also enjoyed the sermon, but Frank seemed to make a full 360 degree turn from his old way of life. Although she had genuinely repented and started to follow Christ, she knew that Frank was on a different level.

Not long after Frank arrived home, he gave Grandma a call. She told him that she was cooking a full course meal for him and Tameka. He confirmed their visit and told her that they would arrive in about an hour. Upon arrival, they couldn't help but notice the sweet-smelling aroma coming from the kitchen. They both gave Grandma a hug before she led the way to the dinner table. Tameka pulled out Grandma's and Frank's chairs before they sat down.

Grandma volunteered to say the grace but because Frank was so hungry, it seemed more like a mini-sermon. When she finished, they each enjoyed the good food that GOD had provided and Grandma had carefully prepared. For about a good 15 minutes, the only noise was the sound of the forks scraping the bottom of the plates. Out of nowhere Grandma said, "I really miss Tarrance and Malik." Although Frank was trying to block this topic out of his head, he knew that Grandma talking about this would essentially be therapeutic.

He then replied, "I can't even begin to understand how you feel, Grandma, but I do know that it's natural to feel as you do." Tameka joined in, "I'm sure Tarrance's soul is at rest."

Grandma didn't want to speculate so she said, "You don't know how bad I hope that he's at rest but that's for GOD to judge and now Malik is in over his head. I never asked you, Frank, but can you tell me what led up to all of this?"

Frank gulped and thought carefully before he answered, "We got into a fight with another gang and thought nothing of it and when we went to the funeral, they ambushed us." He answered elusively, trying not to get into too much detail. He didn't actually tell the truth but technically he didn't lie either.

Grandma reacting like a prosecutor asked, "Did y'all boys sell drugs and kill people?" She and Tameka listened attentively as Frank reminisced about how the jury had listened to him a few years ago at his possession trial. "We were involved with a lot of things. The devil really had us deceived."

Grandma wasn't satisfied with the evasive answer. "You didn't answer my question. Did y'all kill and sell drugs?" Frank looked like a crippled bird against a wall, looking at a cat's fangs. "Yea Mama and Tameka, I'm ashamed to admit the things I used to be involved with."

Tameka looked at Frank as she said, "I know GOD forgives you because he knows your heart is pure now." Grandma put her right hand on his lap as she said, "Yea, Babe, GOD forgives you for everything you did before; as a matter of fact, he doesn't even remember it." She continued, "I just don't understand! I can't even count how many nights I prayed for them boys. Now look, one dead at 20, 21 and the other on the run, wanted dead or alive." Frank tried to console Grandma with his words. "It wasn't the lack of praying, Mama, the devil just lured us into his web of deception. He led us into the fast life and I know he had us in a head lock."

Tameka tried to make the conversation more hopeful by saying, "But I know that GOD is gonna call Suga and he's gonna respond."

Grandma continued with tears in her eyes, "I hope so and I also hope them police don't kill him too."

Ironically, this topic answered the dreaded question for Grandma but it also gave her a higher admiration for Frank's conversion to the Christian lifestyle. They spent the rest of the evening talking about a variety of things. Frank had known Grandma for many years but for the first time, he actually called her Mama and really felt it. Tameka also felt as if Grandma was a third grandmother to her. At around 9:30 p.m., Tameka and Frank mutually decided to leave. Tameka stopped off at Frank's house for about 30 minutes, then she went home. Another muggy Houston night was history, never to return again.

CHAPTER 7

END TIMES

At 12:00 p.m. Monday afternoon, Suga finally reached his home away from home. After he got his backpack, he called the directory to get his aunt's phone number. When he got it, he called. The voice on the other end was deep with a heavy southern accent.

"Hello, can I speak to Mark?" Suga said (Mark was his cousin's name).

"This me, who's this asking?"

Suga sounded relieved. "Yo man, this your cousin Malik."

Mark was happy to hear from his cousin. "Malik! What's up? What, it's been about five years I ain't saw you."

Suga said, "About that long." He continued, "Say cuz, where you live at from this Greyhound station?" Mark replied "Which one? The one on Hibiscus Street?"

"Yea."

"Be in the front in about 20 minutes."

"Thanks, man."

In 19 minutes, Mark was in the front of the bus station. He immediately recognized his cousin and honked the car horn.

ALLEY CAT SLICK

When Suga realized that it was Mark, he smiled and jogged to the car. They embraced each other once they were both seated in the car. As Mark drove away, he asked, "So what happened to Tarrance?" This was the first time Suga had talked about seeing his cousin's death so it came out slowly. "Man, we had some beef with some Spanish dudes and while we were at a homie's funeral, they started blasting on us. The next thing I knew, three brothers were dead, one paralyzed and me and Solo were the only ones' left standing."

Mark was curious and asked, "How many of them was there and how they knew y'all was at your dog's funeral?" The faces were vivid in Suga's mind. "There were about four of them but they had automatic weapons and it looks like one of the niggas they killed had back stabbed us."

"So did y'all get those vatoes back?"

Suga felt a deep burning in his chest as he said, "Naw man, they fled the country but before I die, I know that I'm gonna see them again. And when I do, I'm not responsible for anything that may happen."

Mark continued to question his younger cousin. "So what brings you to this part of town?"

"I got into a gun fight with some well-connected people and now I'm a fugitive, refusing to go down easy."

Mark said in a low voice, "Don't worry cousin, you're in my town and I got your back now."

Although it was a Monday, Tameka had the day off. She was doing some packing up in preparation of moving in with Frank after they got married (less than a week away). Around 2:30 p.m., her door bell rang unexpectedly. Tameka debated with herself whether to answer since no one knew that it was her day off except her fiancé. She decided to answer it as it could be an emergency. To her amazement, she saw Derek there with some red roses. She didn't know whether to be upset or glad to see her ex-boyfriend. Derek asked if he could come in and again she reasoned to herself before giving an answer. Finally she said yes, vowing to herself not to succumb to any possible temptation. When Derek came in, he closed the door, gave Tameka the roses and tried to give her a peck on her lips. Before he could successfully fulfill the move, she moved away and handed back the roses. Politely she said, "Thank you for the gesture but I'm already taken, so I can't possibly take the roses, much less kiss you."

Derek looked disappointed but was not quite ready to give up. "I'm sorry. I wasn't trying to impose but I figured that a kiss and roses are nothing, being that we have history with each other."

Tameka stared at the wall as she said, "I know. That's exactly why we shouldn't start anything that we can't finish."

Derek reached for Tameka's hand and said, "Why can't we finish, Tameka? I definitely won't object."

Tameka, sensing that the devil was trying to trap her in a snare, was now more determined than ever to pass the test. She was blunt, "Look Derek, I'm engaged to marry Tank on Saturday. We had our time in the past, but that was then and this is now ,and now I'm madly in love with Frank." Derek smirked as he said, "Who? That crippled nigga? What can he possibly do for you? I heard that he can barely stand. What's wrong with you? Have you lost your mind?"

Tameka usually could control her temper but she became infuriated at this. "Let me tell you something. I'm not in love with his shell, I'm in love with him. If you trusted in GOD, you would understand what I'm saying. We both gave our lives to GOD and as a result, I have finally experienced true love in the presence of our heavenly Father, Christian friends and a future husband. You see, the body counts for very little in comparison to the person inside the body. So I'll boldly and happily admit that I'm in love with a crippled man. But if you knew him like I do, then you wouldn't have the audacity to call Frank a cripple, because he's still actually good at what he does."

Derek looked at her in disgust before saying, "I don't know what you call him but to me and everyone else he's just another crippled nigga. But if that's your choice, I just hope you'll stick to it and don't even look my way when you see me blow up, because you've had your chance and you blew it."

As he was walking out of the door, Tameka confirmed her decision to him verbally. "Don't worry, Derek, I'll stick to my decision, and by the way, I wouldn't leave Frank for the world."

Tameka was surprised at herself. Not that she didn't love Frank, but at the fact that she had defended him wholeheartedly against Derek, of all people. This really made her realise that she was ready to marry her ex-secret lover. She could have easily folded under pressure and given into the wiles of the devil, but she successfully overcame the trial thrown at her. Even though she had handled the situation so well, it wasn't as easy as it seemed. Remember, she's still human and the flesh of a believer sometimes lusts. Although she succeeded over this particular test, she was wise enough to know that in order to continually defeat the devil, she had to fellowship with other believers. So she paid Grandma an unexpected visit and shared this situation with her.

When Tameka told Grandma of her trial, Grandma was pleased to hear how well she had handled it. Grandma also told Tameka that she was wise to pay her a visit, because she said strength comes in numbers. Grandma then changed the subject and told Tameka that the previous night, she had had a disturbing dream. When she told Tameka this, she instantaneously forgot about her trial with Derek. They prayed and read some scriptures together before Tameka left to pick up Frank from work.

Frank was already waiting downstairs when Tameka arrived. As usual, they gave each other hugs and kisses in greeting but for some unknown reason, Frank sensed she was squeezing him so tight that his blood circulation seemed to be cut off. He asked her while they were driving off, "What was that for? It seems as if you're seeing me for the first time in years!"

Tameka, watching the car in front of her, said, "That's for being you and it does sort of seem like I haven't seen you in years."

Frank put his hand on her knees. "I can live with that, but I hope you feel the same way after we're married for years with children and grandchildren."

She smiled while she said, "Yea, I will. I just hope the feeling will be mutual."

Before they went home, the two decided to evangelize in the projects of Forrest City, known as a gang-plagued area infamous for drugs and senseless crimes. Shortly after they arrived, a group of hoodlums walked towards Frank and Tameka. Frank began preaching even though it was evident that they weren't paying much attention. One of the hoodlums shouted, "Man, you better get out of here, talking all that junk!"

Frank calmly said, "The words I speak aren't my own, but the Holy words of The Most High."

Another hoodlum said, "We're gonna give you a minute to get out of here. After that, we're gonna do anything that comes to mind and I know that we'll have fun with that ol' gal over there!"

Frank was stubborn but not stupid. Even though he didn't want to leave at their threats, he didn't want to expose Tameka to any harm. They weren't even there for ten minutes before they were driven out of the projects.

Frank wanted to go to another area and witness but Tameka convinced him to go home. When they were home, Tameka told

Frank about the incident with Derek. Frank was irate to say the least. He hadn't got this upset ever since he got saved, but I guess what happened at Forrest City had pushed him over the edge. He was mad at Derek for disrespecting him like that, and he was mad at Tameka for letting him into her house. He lost control; he was yelling at Tameka and pushing over objects in his house. After a few minutes of this, Tameka began to weep. When Frank realized that she was sobbing, he regained his composure and calmed down.

He apologized to Tameka for his temper tantrum and complimented her on her reaction to Derek. He finally opened up to her and told her that his reaction was mainly because of his frustration over being partially paralyzed. She had suspected that he might be depressed over his loss, but because he concealed it so well, she didn't think much of it. Although Frank and Tameka were saved, they knew very well that they were still susceptible to sin in their life. As a result, they prayed together and separately for the remainder of the day.

When Suga woke up the next morning, Mark was already up and on the phone. Suga overheard his cousin in the next room arguing with the person on the other end of the phone. By the sound of the argument, it seemed as if Mark was getting worked up over an unpaid debt. He threatened the person before he slammed the phone down. Suga then walked into his cousin's room and asked him what the commotion was about. Mark answered vaguely and told Suga that it was a small problem, nothing that he should worry about. Suga didn't worry but he kept a mental note of it.

After the two ate and dressed, Suga followed Mark to what he thought was a friend's house. Mark told Suga to wait in the car while he made a quick stop. About five minutes later, Mark ran out of the house and hopped into the car. When he was driving away, a guy came out of the house cursing at Mark and Suga. Suga, noticeably upset, asked Mark, "Yo man, what's going on? How come that guy is cussing at you?"

Mark kept his eyes straight on the road while he said "Man, this cat owed me some money so I had to collect it."

Suga got mad and said, "Come on now, you know that I'm on the run and you brought me here!"

Mark said in a nonchalant manner, "Don't worry cousin, I already told you that you're safe with me."

Suga then realized that if he wanted to lay low, his cousin Mark was the wrong person to be with.

They stopped off at a bar and ordered two vodkas on the rocks. While they were drinking, Mark said, "Alright cousin, I'm gonna let you know the deal." He looked around before he continued. "This morning I was arguing with one of my customers, oh yea, I sell dope. I know that I should have told you before, but you know that ain't the type of thing that I voluntarily tell people."

Suga moved closer to Mark. "What kind of drugs do you sell?"

"Anything that my customers need, I provide for them. Hey, I know that you're on the run and you probably want to stay on the down low, but if you're interested, I have a position available. It would be good to have family on my team, you know, someone that I could turn my back to." Suga took a big gulp before he said, "I don't know man. I need a little time to thing this over."

Mark said, "Alright" and ordered two more drinks.

The next day at work, Frank could barely concentrate because he was thinking of how the gangsters had treated him in Forrest City the day before. As his work day came to an end, he decided to call Tameka at her work and tell her that he wouldn't need her to pick him up after work. She seemed kind of curious to find out how he was coming home, but she didn't want to come off as a jealous girl, so she kept her peace. She just told him that she would be at his apartment when he got there.

After work, Frank called a taxi-cab to take him to Bluepoints Mall. The mall was busy on that particular day. All the better, Frank thought; there would be more people to witness to. He shared the gospel (good news) of Christ to everyone who passed him. After being there about an hour, some Bluepoints posse members passed him. They walked over to him and began to ridicule him. He tried to ignore their insults but they were insistent on bothering him. They threatened to physically harm him.

Frank simply replied, "Do whatever makes you happy but I want you to know that although you can kill my body, you can't kill my soul." At this, Detrick (one of the leaders) gave him a solid shot to his face which knocked him to the ground. About five minutes later, Frank regained consciousness and found himself in an ambulance, being brought to the hospital. He tried to resist medical attention, but the paramedics had to make sure that he was stable before they allowed him to go home. He wasn't severely harmed except for a bloody nose and lips and a mild concussion. The paramedics asked him questions like, was this a gang-related incident and did he know the perpetrators. After they treated him, they let him call Tameka who took him home.

Tameka was worried for Frank's safety more than he was. When he got home, she pampered him to the point that he had to tell her that he wasn't a baby. Shortly after they arrived home, there was a knock at the door. When Tameka answered it, she was surprised to see two plain clothes detectives. They asked to talk to Frank, so she let them in.

When they saw Frank, they noticed his swollen lips and nose. One of the detectives said, "I can see that you're still affiliated with your gang, what do you guys call yourselves? Isn't it Willowcreek Posse?"

Frank quietly answered, "I don't gang-bang anymore." The fat detective sarcastically said, "I can see that."

Frank, knowing that he was referring to his swollen lips, said, "I got this for preaching about Christ." He laughed to himself. "Can you believe that people hate GOD so much that they'll practically kill you for doing what's right in GOD's sight?"

The slim detective said, "I know the code of the streets, thou shalt not cooperate with the police, but we're here on different business." The fat detective took over, "It's about your friend Malik. You probably know him better as, (he looked in his notebook) Suga. I understand your loyalty to your friend but remember that he attempted to murder four people and the worst thing about it is that one of the persons is a decorated officer. Now if you're a good friend you'll understand that his life is in danger because now we know that he'll shoot. So do your friend a favor and tell us where he is."

At that Frank said, "Believe me when I say that I don't know where he is."

The slim detective smiled before he said, "We kind of knew you were going to say that. To be honest with you, we're trying to prevent you from having another dead friend but it's your call."

Frank again said, "Sorry officers, I can't help you." Before the detectives left, they gave him their cards with their names and numbers and told him to call if he had a change of mind.

Later on that night, Suga and Mark were at a birthday party for one of Mark's friends. He introduced Suga to a few of his friends at the party. Suga noticed that they all had respectable wardrobes and almost all of them were accompanied by beautiful women. After Mark gave Suga a tour of the townhouse, he again posed the question to him, "Yo Malik, me and one of my men is headed down south to Miami to take care of some business. I want to know if you've thought about my offer."

Suga noticed one of the girls staring at him. "Yea, man, I've given it some thought, and I would like that."

Mark shook his hands as he said, "Good decision cuz! We're gonna represent for the family."

Suga agreed. "Yea, the family."

Deep down inside, Suga really wanted to change his lifestyle, but it's not that easy to come out of. I guess one can say that it's an addictive lifestyle. It's hard to be used to having money and all of sudden being broke. Don't get me wrong, I'm making no excuses for Suga's decision, but looking at it from his perspective, I can understand.

The two of them stayed at the party all night long until early the next morning. By the looks of it, Suga and the girl who was staring at him (her name was Tabitha), were getting along well with each other. Mark was busy flirting with at least three different girls who seemed to follow him around like groupies. Suga then knew with certainty that his cousin was a major hustler, also known as a heavy hitter.

When they left the party, Mark told him that they would be leaving for Miami later on that evening and would stay there for two to three days. Suga asked, "So what are we gonna do down there?"

Mark answered, "I have some workers down there and they need a few kilos of powder but I have a contact that's coming from Jamaica with a few pounds of herb on the following day. So basically, we're gonna bring things over there and in return, we'll bring back things over here. You see, cousin, I'm about to build an empire here but like I said, it would be sweeter with family on my side."

They again shook hands before Suga verified his decision. "You know, I'm down with that, Baby. As a matter of fact, this is for Playa, another true soldier in the family." Mark agreed also and they made a dirty covenant with each other.

Later on that same day, Mark and Suga packed some clothes and picked up Rodney (Mark's partner in crime) and headed down south to Miami. Rodney was an upper-middle-class, white American from a respectable family. It was a good cover because Rodney was one of those kids who dreamed about being poor and from the ghetto, so Mark thought it would look less suspicious if he had Rodney to do the more risky work. From the first sight of Rodney, Suga wasn't impressed with him. Mark introduced the two as soon as they drove off. Rodney asked Suga, just trying to make conversation, "Where you from?"

Suga answered the question rudely, "I thought you knew I was brought here from Africa on a ship by your peoples, and now y'all distribute drugs in my area and I ain't got no other choice but to sell drugs for a living. Now you know where I'm from. Any more questions sir?"

Rodney noticed the hostility, "I'm sorry I asked."

Mark noticed it also. "Say Suga, you ain't got to go off on him like that. Man! Look here, I don't hang around no flakes. Yea, Rodney's white but believe me when I say that he's down for the cause."

Suga looked at his cousin and said, "Alright, I'ma take your word for that." He then apologized to Rodney and shook his hand.

It took a few hours to reach Miami and in that space of time, Suga realized that Rodney was alright. He said, "Yo Rodney, you're alright for a white boy."

Rodney answered back jokingly, "You're alright for a black boy too." They all laughed at the rhetoric.

When they reached Miami, Mark chose a hotel along Miami Beach to stay at. They all got separate rooms and as soon as they packed up, they went club hopping along the beach. Of course they met a couple of young ladies who were willing to help them spend their money and after, they returned to their rooms for some extra curricular activities.

Mark woke up first and immediately he called the supposed purchaser of the drugs. He set up a time and place for the illegal transaction to take place. Then he woke up the other two.

When it was time to do the first phase of their operation, Malik gave Rodney the merchandise and told him to carry it out as earlier discussed. Rodney rented a car; Mark also rented a car for him and his cousin to follow Rodney and be his lookout guys. When Rodney met with one guy, another guy with him seemed to be intoxicated out of his mind. Although the other guy seemed paranoid, the transaction unraveled smoothly and without any unfortunate incidents. After they had made the score, the three went partying which was by now a normal custom. Even though people may think the gangster lifestyle is glamorous, it really isn't. When you really think about it, there's only partying, women, drug abuse and gathering of material items. Nothing too exciting. A life without purpose is a shallow life. Although they may gather some possessions, they will never be totally satisfied.

The wedding day finally made its way around and there was no way to avoid it. Even though traditionally it's a nerve-wracking day for the groom and bride to be, Frank and Tameka seemed to be relaxed. Frank was at his home, accompanied by a few of the brethren from the Church, while Tameka was at Grandma's apartment with some of the sisters.

The night before, the brethren had given Frank a bachelor party to celebrate his last night as a single man. It was simple but nice. They ate some tasty food, talked about their experiences as God-faring husbands, and basically carried on as a group of high school students. Like I said, it was simple; there was no liquor, naked women, or obscene jokes but they all enjoyed the evening. A few of the bachelors even stayed the night to assist Frank on his special day in the morning.

Tameka also had a pleasurable night before her wedding. Although it wasn't technically called a bachelorette party, it was as exciting as her future husband's night had been. There was food, talking, joking, recipe sharing and more girl things. Unlike the men, all of the ladies went home after a certain time, but Tameka stayed at Grandma's house for the night.

The wedding was to take place at 1:00 p.m., so at 12:30, both Frank and Tameka were at the Church getting ready to give their lives in Holy Matrimony to each other. At this time, butterflies began to enter each of their stomachs, but they knew that they had to overcome the nervousness. It's as if their spirits were one because although they were separated, they both said brief prayers at the exact same time.

The time Frank had anxiously waited for, finally arrived. One of the elders in the Church escorted Tameka down the aisle and led her to Frank. He looked in awe as he beheld her beauty in her wedding gown. While the Pastor was giving the vows, they looked into each other's eyes as if to say from this point on they would be one, inseparable and the decision they had made was now irrevocable. After they exchanged rings, the Pastor said, "I now pronounce you husband and wife. Frank, you may now kiss the bride." Although Frank had kissed Tameka numerous times in the past, it was as if he was a teenager giving a kiss for the first time.

When the ordeal was over, Tameka threw her bouquet of flowers to an eager maiden and the couple got into their limousine.

When they made it to the banquet hall, people were already there celebrating. The interesting thing about the attendance at the reception was the fact that half of the people were believers of Jesus Christ and the other half non-believers. There were people from the Church, some of Frank's old friends, as well as Tameka's family in attendance. If you think about it, that was an unusual crowd. Christians, concerned family members and hardcore gangsters. Although a large number of people in the crowd were non-believers, Frank and Tameka still chose to keep the reception in a Christian atmosphere. One of the ways they did this was by leading the reception off by saying a prayer. They also had a contemporary Christian band that disc-jockied, and also the only alcohol that was served was some red wine. Everyone ate and was merry. The kids played while the grown-ups danced and gave the newlyweds gifts. They received many useful gifts, but the most cherished one was given by Frank's employer. Before he presented it to Frank and Tameka, he said, "I pray that GOD blesses your marriage and shows you guys wonderful things like he's shown me and my wife. I also appreciate the fact that you, Frank, have been a committed worker and to show my gratitude, this is for your wife." He handed Frank an unsealed envelope. Before Frank looked inside to see what it was, he thanked his boss and then saw that it was two tickets to Hawaii for a week's stay. After it sunk in, he hugged his boss and innocently gave him a brotherly kiss on the cheek. His boss jokingly said after receiving the kiss, "Hey, let's not get carried away! After all, we're both married men."

Frank and Tameka were understandably happy over the day, but this gift was the icing on the cake. The ticket was for the next day at 1:30 p.m.. One by one the crowd began to disperse until Tameka, Grandma and Frank were left. Before they dropped Grandma home, Frank told her that she had been one of the strongest inspirations in his life and he really appreciated her influence on him. Well, needless to say, Frank and Tameka rushed home to legitimize their marriage by coming together as one.

The next morning, Frank and Tameka packed their clothes in a suit case, made a few calls to say good-bye and were off to catch their plane and to celebrate their honeymoon.

At the same time as Frank and Tameka were boarding the plane for Hawaii, Suga, Mark and Rodney had to make a transaction with one of Rodney's contacts. They conspired to sell the contact $45,000 worth of cocaine. When they arrived, Rodney made sure that all of the merchandise was in a suit case and went to meet the purchaser. He had done business with this contact a few times over the last year, so he chose to drive in the car with Mark and Suga.

When they met up with the guy, the contact seemed to be nervous, but Rodney overlooked it and proceeded. Rodney asked him, "Do you have all the money?"

The guy answered back, "You said $45,000, right?" "Yes."

After they had made the exchange, they both went their separate ways. Then it all happened, as if in slow motion - drug enforcement agents came from everywhere. They surrounded the car with automatic weapons in Mark and Suga's faces. They also tackled Rodney onto the ground. Although they didn't have time to think, they all knew that they had been set up by Rodney's contact. In fact, the police knew everything that the two gangsters had done in the last year.

Initially they didn't know where Suga fit in, but after they got his fingerprints, they realized that they had got a bigger score than they had bargained for. The state of Texas extradited Suga in order to make him stand trial for his crimes. Back in Florida, Suga attained numerous charges. In Texas, the prospect didn't look any better.

After all the adventure that the gang life carried, all six of the Willocreek members had faced some kind of consequence for their participation. Although Frank converted to Christianity and left the game, his body would always be affected by the earlier choices he had made. Playa and Pop were killed as a result of their actions. Solo received a 20- to 45-year sentence for three counts of attempted murder. Suga received a 30- to 60-year sentence in Texas and a10- to 20-year sentence in Florida. Pookie, although he tried to be lukewarm as far as the gang was concerned, was also killed. Frank and Tameka slowly but surely prospered in life. They eventually had two children, a boy and a girl.

THE END

Because of the Blood of Jesus Christ, I am more than a conqueror. To God be all the glory.

I did it!

CONDENSED EBONICS DICTIONARY

Broke- having little or no money

357- murder

5.0.- police

Alley Cat Slick- a ghetto youth that's a smooth operator

Audi- same as dip

Ballin- to live lavishly; to play sports (usually basketball)

Beef- differences between 2 parties which have the potential to escalate to violence

Bid- spending a substantial time in jail

Big Willy- similar to boss player

Blast- to shoot a gun

Blazing- shooting or smoking marijuana

Bling Bling- flashy accessories; diamonds

Blitz- intoxicated

Blow up- to rise in status

Booty- buttocks

Boss player- a hustler on top of his or her game

Bout it- willing to do

Break out- to start to, or to dip

Broad- female

Bumping- loud music
Burner- same as heat
Cap you- to shoot you
Cat- a person
Cheddar- money
Cheese- same as cheddar
Chick- female
Chicken- female
Chill-to lounge or take easy
Chill out- take it easy
Ching Ching- making money
Cowboy- an uncontrollable individual that's trigger happy
Craps- a dice game 7/11 style
Crazy- not to be messed with
Creeping- moving discreetly, (usually refers to someone cheating)
Crunk- hype
Cuss- to swear or to use vulgar language
Cuz- a word similar in meaning to brother
Dame- a girl or female
Dead that-to put to an end
Dime piece- a beautiful girl
Dip- to leave
Dog- same as homie
Dookie- feces
Dope-good; drugs
Down low- same as creeping
Eat your food- to physically harm

Ends- same as cheese

Essay- a latin person, (usually a Mexican)

Fa real- not lying

Feel me- to relate

Flasher-a person that goes nude in public

Flashy- flamboyant dresser,

Flaunt- to show

Flip- to lose composure

Floss- to show off

Fly- nice

Fool- similar to nigga

Freak- a promiscuous person

Free styling-the act of rapping without writing it down

G's- friends

Gat- same as heat

Get at me- similar to hit me up

Ghost- same as dip

Good look- something is good

Good looking out- thank you

Grimy- same as shady

Grip- same as cheddar; a gun

Gully- same as gutter

Gung-ho- willing and eager to shoot a gun

Gutter- a poverty stricken area

Heat- gun

Herb- a clown, someone that isn't taken seriously; geek;marijuana

Hit me up- call me back

Heavy hitter- similar to boss player

Holla- to give a greeting

Homeboy- a guy

Homegirl- a girl

Homes- similar to nigga

Homie- same as my nigga

Hood- neighborhood

Hot- same as fly

Hotside-to act too good; to think to highly of yourself

Jack(ed)- to rob or the act of getting robbed

Jakes- police

Jit- child

Jit-a-bug- same as jit

Joe Grind- a guy that specializes in having affairs

Keep your head up- stay encouraged

Kick it- same as chill

Kicks- sneakers

Kin- relative

Kin folk- same as homie

Knocked- getting arrested

KrippNigg- crippled nigga

Lay low- same as chilling; to hide out

Little man- same as jit

Live- similar to ballin

Loc- gangster

Lost it- crazy

Low blow- experiencing an unfortunate incident

Machine- automatic gun

Mack- same as boss player

Mad- a lot of

Mean-mugging- staring at someone with anger

M.O.B.- money over broads

Mommy- a girlfriend; a mother

Moving backward- doing things wrong

My bad- I'm sorry

My fault- I'm sorry

My nigga- a close friend

Nigga- (not to be mistaken with the word "nigger") a male; black people(a term of endearment)

Off- to kill

Off the head-the act of rapping without writing it down

Off the hinges- same as crunk

Off the hook-spectacular, magnificent, great

Off the hook- same as crunk

OG- original gangster, a gangster with street credibility's

On my face- having no money

On point- sharp, accurate

One- peace

One Tom- police

Packing- to be armed

Peel your cap- shoot you

Phat- same as fly

Popping- same as crunk

Potna- same as homie

Props- to give respect to

Punk niggas- having little or no respect towards that individual

Ranking- the act of talking about someone in a competitive way

Reefer- marijuana

Ride- a car; the act of retaliation

Rider- same as boss player

Riding- the act of retaliation; to live large

Ripped- same as blitz

Road dog- similar to homeboy

Rolling- the act of retaliation; to drive in a car

Run- everyone has to answer to

Running it- to be on top of things

Scoot over- move over

Shady- someone that can't be trusted

Shine- being together; on point

Sharp-good dresser

Shorty- a girl; a young person

Shout out- acknowledgement

Slick- smooth operator, elusive, nice dresser

Slippery-elusive, slick

Slipping- to act careless

Slow your roll- to think before you act

Sorry- worthless

Stacked- a sexy girl

Starving like Marvin- extremely hungry

Static- trouble

Steelo- what one is known for

Stogey- cigarette

Struggle- (usually referring) to the plight of the black race

Swig- to drink liquor
Tele- hotel
The bomb- same as fly
The law- police
Thick- a sexy girl; to be strong
Tight- being close to; stingy; looks good
Tipsy- being drunk
Torn- intoxicated
Trife- same as shady
Trigger happy- eager to shoot a gun
Trip- same as flip
Tripping- to joke; same as flip
Twisted- mixed up
Unknown Shadow Dwellers- smooth operators
Vinna- about to
What's up?- how are you doing
Whip- car
Wifey- girlfriend
Word- not lying
Word is bond- a promise
Word up- not lying
Wounded Warrior- original bad boy; sole survivor
You dig- do you understand
Young blood- same as jit
Young buck- same as jit

ISBN 1425107346